THE STORY HOUSE

The Cottage, and other short stories

By

Pauline Lewis

Illustrations by
Rachel M. Hare

MOORLEYS
Print & Publishing

ISBN 978 0 86071 628 0

© Copyright 2010 Pauline Lewis

All rights reserved. No part of this publication may be reproduced, stored in a retrieval system, or transmitted, in any form or by any means, electronic, mechanical, photocopying, recording or otherwise, without the prior written permission of the publishers.

There is no restriction on the public reading of these stories in the context of a devotional meeting.

British Library Cataloguing in Publication Data.
A catalogue record for this book is available from the British Library.

Cover photo:
© Adam Fraise - Shutterstock® Images

MOORLEYS
Print & Publishing
23 Park Road, Ilkeston, Derbyshire DE7 5DA
Tel/Fax: 0115 932 0643 email: info@moorleys.co.uk

CONTENTS

Introduction

1. The Cottage 5
2. That Cat 8
3. What Odds? 11
4. The Lighted Window 15
5. The Special Clinic 19
6. Ben's Bunker 27
7. The Bluebell 31
8. The Island 35
9. Love & East Enders 43
10. The Passing Place 47
11. Fantastic 53
12. The Christmas Gift 57
13. East West, Home's Best 63
14. Life is for Living 67
15. Shepherd Lad 71
16. Spring of Joy 75
17. Village Hermit 79
18. Man's Best Friend 83
19. Fifty Years On 87

THE STORY HOUSE

Introduction

Somewhere in the heart of Wales you may have come across the Story House. I longed to bring children into this quaint building, with its strange shapes and smells. We could imagine ourselves in some dark cabin, timbers creaking around us, sailing to a new world; or maybe besieged in a castle, looking out through the misted windows for our delivering army.

I'm told that the strange little house is no longer there, but I know that in the recesses of my mind I have found my own story house. Not many of the tales I have gathered here are true, though most have been based on real people and situations. Some were written as prayers, some as modern day parables, and others as sheer fantasy, but all in the assurance that God can enter into any situation. He is a God of joy who wants us to be part of his story and enjoy his happy ending.

Having gathered them together, I pray that as you dip into them you will enjoy and be blessed.

Pauline Lewis 2009

THE COTTAGE

Hannah joined her mother as she sat, watching the work going on at the cottage across the valley.

'I remember it as a happy home,' Kay told her. 'A farm labourer he was. When his wife died, old Jo went to pieces - neglected himself, and the old place.' Somehow the tumble down cottage had seemed like her life, since they had diagnosed her mysterious illness, a picture of hopelessness.

'It's as if it's coming back to life, Mum.' Hannah seemed to understand. 'Look! Those extra windows, - and that room, to catch all the sun. They're putting in a bathroom too, and a pump to bring water from the well.'

'As long as it's not just a holiday cottage,' Kay sighed.

With watching work across the valley, she became aware of the changing of the seasons. The children were gathering blackberries when a furniture van lumbered up the narrow lane.

Hannah didn't drag her feet to join her mother these days. 'They're quite young, Mum. At least, she is. They say he's been ill - come down here for peace and quiet.'

'I didn't have to move to find that, did I?' There was bitterness in her mother's response. Then, 'Maybe they'll start a family. It would be wonderful if it became a happy family home again. I can just see it, all white washed, with roses and clematis covering the walls and children in the garden. Oh look – they're coming to the door now. I wish I could see well.'

'I hope the Doves have got nothing to hide,' her husband laughed, fixing a stand for her binoculars. Everyone called them this since the cottage had been renamed 'Dove Spring.'

5

Now, while Hannah regaled her with gossip from around the village, Kay told of all she had seen from her bedroom window.

'Larry, could you find my easel? I've got an itch to do some painting.' Her husband was delighted to see his wife taking an interest in life again. Dare he suggest taking her out in the car? She might accept being pushed in a wheel chair.

It did Kay so much good to be driven down to the bay, and feel the salt wind in her hair. She did a few sketches of the cliffs and the fishing boats, but mostly she painted her valley, especially the cottage. She laughed at old Sal, picking watercress from the brook to take to the 'Doves'. She would come away with her bag full, for she lived off those who were vulnerable to her hard luck stories.

It was Sal who started the rumour that a little dove was on the way. The word spread and Kay was imagining children playing by the well. When the nurse told her there wasn't any hope of it, for a couple of days she could not get out of bed. Her own progress seemed to be linked with the home across the valley.

But then it was Saturday and Hannah came upstairs to coax her.
'Mum, I'm sure I saw a kingfisher, down by the brook. Do try to come and see.' Patiently she helped her mother into her chair then wheeled her across to the window. She knelt quietly beside her and then, there it was, a jewelled flash of hope.

The next time Hannah came in her mother was painting. She had Mrs Dove sitting on her doorstep, while the walls of the cottage were awash with a rich purple clematis. 'That's grown quickly,' she teased. She had told her mother that they had planted one, along with some roses.

Through the long golden summer a succession of visitors came to Dove Spring. The old home had certainly come to life. Another summer came and went then, with the falling of the leaves came sad news. Mr Dove was in a deep depression. Just before Christmas, the cottage was left empty, and Kay once more had taken to her bed.

'Andy has been in and lit the fire. They must be coming back, Mum.' It didn't take long for word to spread. Yes. Mrs Dove was back. But where was he? What hope of a family now? Could a young woman survive in such an isolated spot without a car, and they, her nearest neighbours, half a mile away?

'Mum, guess what? She's teaching at our school. Comes with us on the school bus.'

Through that long cold winter, they heard stories of their solitary dove; how the farmer up the valley has rescued her when she was snow bound; how old Sal, instead of coming to beg, was proving a friend in need; and with the Spring came the children – young Barbara, the gardener's daughter first, then her friends joined her. Roses and clematis were growing up her wall, and the children…. Kate was busy again with her paintbrush.

Sometimes she thought she heard singing. That must be a very special spring. Kay listened and wondered. Perhaps she has faith that her dove will come back to its nest, and then little doves be on their way. She had waited a long time for her Hannah and felt for the young woman.

The years passed swiftly. Mrs Dove had her own car now, a permanent position at the school, and they had brought electricity up their valley. Was she better off without him? Then it was rumoured that he had been seen. There was another car by the gate. Stories abounded. Kay watched and yes, prayed. Surely now he would stay and share the contentment his wife had found, and her picture become reality.

'He *is* back,' she told Hannah. 'I saw them in the orchard together, and he's been digging in their vegetable patch. But what's happened to the clematis? It should have been in bloom by now. Surely they haven't dug it up?'

'It's the wash they used on the walls. The clematis doesn't like it, Andy says.' Hannah had had to ask. It seemed so important to her mother. 'It happened before; grew up to window level, then died. He thought it was a gonner, but amazingly, a couple of years later, it sprang up again. But he says it's gone for good this time. – The roses are surviving though, Mum.'

'Mrs Dove has given in her notice, Mum, and the cottage is up for sale.' Kay wasn't as devastated by the news as she would have been when she was a prisoner in her bedroom. With the stair lift and her electric buggy she had some independence. All the same, she was sad. She couldn't help thinking of this lovely young woman, having to bury her hopes of a family as she returned to city life to care for an elderly husband. What had happened to her hopes and dreams; more than that, her faith?

'Hannah, where's my easel?' Watching the evening sun light up the little cottage, Kay noticed that the walls were a splash of purple. The clematis had found courage to rise again, and claim its territory. As she painted, she felt a quiet assurance that all was well with the Doves.

'The Cottage'

Branscombe was the village to which my sister and her husband escaped after he had had a breakdown. It would make a wonderful setting for a novel. But as I pondered I found it was a true story I was writing, of 'the Doves' anyway. I do not know who was living in the farm across the valley.

THAT CAT

I've always had an aversion to cats. Maybe I inherited it from my father. He reckoned he was allergic to them.

The trouble was, the children loved Candy. It was convenient because we were learning the sound 'c'. He was the caretaker's cat. And he was always wandering into our classroom. Lots of 'c' sounds there, but not enough to endear him to me.

Why did he call him Candy? He wasn't like anything we buy from the sweet shop. We decided to ask him, when he brought the milk in.

'Well you see, my wife decided to call her Candlewick, because she likes to play with the tassels on her candlewick bedspread, but that was rather a long name for a little cat, and anyway, when she holds up her little tail it looks like candy floss, so that is what we call her.'

That was a fun reason, but still I insisted, - 'Please, Mr Jackson, keep him out of our classroom.'

'Trouble is Miss' – how I hate being called Miss, though being called Miss Sniff instead of Smith is even worse. If I don't get married soon I'll have to think about deed poll.

'Trouble is,' he continued, '- he's a she, by the way - She doesn't know she belongs to us. She thinks she just allows us to live in her house, and the school is all part of her domain. I blame the vet. He let her know she was a queen. Anyway Miss, I'll do my best.'

His best wasn't good enough. Can you imagine the commotion when, having gathered the children for a story I went to sit down. There was a terrible yowling and my lovely quiet class was in uproar. I had nearly sat on Candy. At last, to their sorrow, Queen Candy was outside the door.

'Oh, Miss, she was trying to make your cushion warm for you,' they assured me. I had to accept their explanation, though I was not convinced.

Worse was to come. There, - it must have been deliberate, for it was right beside my chair, - was a mouse. The trouble was, I couldn't bring myself to dispose of it, and the children had arrived before I could get hold of the caretaker. They were mixed in their emotions, - pity for the wee mouse, and delight that Candy had brought me a present. 'She wanted to tell you she was sorry, because she frightened you.'

Again, I wasn't convinced. Of course, I should have been grateful. At least it was dead, and had not scared me to death by running out of some dark corner.

But somehow I thought that cat was determined to upset me one way or another, and he, - she I mean, was certainly succeeding.

We had a day or two cat-free, to my relief, but then there were strange rumours going round the school. One of the cleaners was convinced there was a ghost and was threatening to leave her job. But at last the mysterious knockings were located as coming from the games cupboard, and by now Mrs Jackson had noticed that Candy had not come home for her supper. The cleaner was reassured and Candy restored to her home.

I had a word with Mrs Jackson. Perhaps she would be more successful than her husband at keeping pussy indoors.

'I do try, Laura. (At last I was talking to someone who recognised me as a human being, not just a teacher.) But if I shut her up when she thinks she should be out she takes out her chagrin on my best furniture. And anyway, it's Cook. I am sure she must save titbits for her, for she often turns her nose up at her supper.'

Christmas was approaching, and we were busy preparing for yet another Nativity play. Time for our dress rehearsal and so we trailed into the hall to where the box was already in place, waiting for a supply of hay.

I really should not have been surprised that our ubiquitous cat had already showed up. Yes, she had thought our manger was a special place for a pussy cat to have some peace and quiet.

There were squeals of delight as the children discovered the uninvited guest. 'Miss! Miss!' they exclaimed. 'Candy wants to be Jesus. Oh, can she Miss?'

I could see Mr Jackson, who having heard the uproar had guessed his pussy was in trouble again, and was obviously afraid I might have a gun hidden in my pocket, ready to deal with the offender. But by now 'Miss Sniff' – yes, I realised I had been deserving this misnomer by my haughty attitude to one of God's beautiful creatures, - had learned to accept her majesty more graciously.

It happened the day Kevin was brought into our class. We all tried to befriend this tearful little boy, and I had thought he was happily playing with the group in the sand pit. However, when I called them together for milk we suddenly realised he was missing. Panic! No, he was not in the cloakroom, or the toilets. Messengers were sent to the other classrooms. Oh, whatever would we say to his mother if he were lost?

Then we had a message from Mrs Jackson. We tiptoed out to find Kevin sitting by the gate with Candy on his lap.

Mrs Jackson had been about to go out shopping when she saw a little boy trying to climb the, fortunately, locked gates. Then her Candy, whom she had thought left safely indoors, reached up and began to rub herself against his legs. Distracted, the little boy turned to caress her.

9

'So I told him how the little cat cries because she loves going to school and being with the children, and she isn't supposed to go, and now you are crying because you don't want to go.'

I was inspired, and so grateful to this understanding woman.

'Kevin, shall we let Candy come to listen to a story so she won't be sad any more?'

Kevin now was gladly restored to the fold, and yes, Miss Sniff had learned a lesson.

But a cat as Jesus? Surely that was going too far.

'You see, children, Jesus was such a very very special baby because God was his father. No other baby, or doll, is ever good enough to be Jesus, and I certainly think our Candy is not good enough.'

'Oh Miss,' they sighed.

But I continued, 'But the little donkey was there. And the shepherds might have brought some of their baby lambs when they came to see Jesus. And the cows were there, because one of them had let Jesus lie in his manger. And maybe there was a pussy cat too in that stable, so of course Candy can be in our play.'

The play went well, as it invariably does on the big day, but Kevin coming to kneel at the manger with Candy in his arms was undoubtedly the star turn.

It wasn't so long before I changed my name, and no, I did not have to resort to deed poll for at long last my Jim plucked up courage to pop the question. And I hope I have learned my lesson, and that 'Miss Sniff' will not emerge when one of God's lesser creatures intrudes into my life.

'That Cat'

Yes, the caretaker had a cat who delighted the children, though he never intruded into our classroom. This story was an excuse for me to recall the nostalgia of my happy, though sometimes frenetic days teaching in Hoxton.

WHAT ODDS?

On a stack of empty crates, in a basement area of an old house, a bundle of rags gently rose and fell.

The angel was sleeping - but nobody was concerned about him. Angel looked after himself. Besides, Hackstead had other things to worry about.

Angel had not stirred when the first whisper had passed along the street; stalls pushed away; shutters hurriedly erected. 'Sam is out!' From doorways now, Hackstead was waiting, watching; but Angel slept on.

In a corner at the 'Old George,' Jim Potter was taking bets. Not that there was much to bet on. Sam was a 'dead cert,' and Sidney, if he did not run for it, dead 'for cert,' But this would be the fight of a life time, for Jim had been assured that Sidney was prepared to face the enemy, and was even now on his way. Sid Phelps wasn't Hackstead, you see. That put the odds against him to start with. It was the locals who had fed the poison to poor old Sam that it was Sid who had been responsible for him being put away.

In a way, he had been. He admitted it, but he had done it for Sam's good. There had been a building project at the school. Trouble had been brewing for the foreman from the start. Dai Griffiths represented authority, and being an outsider, they resented it. Sidney could see that Sam was to be the pawn they intended to use to do their dirty work.

Sam Huckett could be gentle as a kitten, but the pressure of a brain tumour meant he could be worked up to become a raging bull, and Sidney knew that Sam was 'being worked up'. There could be murder, and Sam the scapegoat. So Sidney had hastened to the doctor, and Sam was put away. Mr Griffiths left Hackstead with nothing worse than a breakdown, the building project incomplete. That had been four years ago.

In the Old George, Sam was being plied with drinks. 'Give it to 'im, Sam lad,' they told him, ''aving you put away like that.' After much back slapping and 'good old Sam'ing, they pushed him out onto the street.

At the other end of the street Sidney Phelps disentangled himself from his wife's arms and closed the door of his carpenter's shop behind him, - and still the Angel slept. Sid knew that his Rosie would never settle away from the bustle of the market and the smell of fish and chips. That was why he had first left the green fields to open his little shop. 'Besides, it is no use running away, love,' he had told her. 'We could be running for the rest of our lives.'

'Go and hide in the church, Sid. Up in the tower,' Rosie had begged now.

'What, and have him come after you and the kids? Not likely, old girl,' and so he had stepped out boldly.

Half way down the street his boldness melted, for he could see his onetime friend approaching, lurching unsteadily, a meat cleaver that he had wrested from the butcher on his way, being waved aloft. Sam's face was flushed, his speech slurred. 'Where are you, Mr Sidney Phelps? I 'eard what you did to me. Put me away, would yer?'

Sidney stood there, enmeshed in the nightmare that had haunted him these last four years. He was paralysed by fear. 'Hello there, Sam!' he tried to call out, but his jaw was trembling, his teeth rattling uncontrollably. This couldn't be happening. It was all so pointless, so stupid.

'Oh God!' He groaned. Even these words wouldn't come out, but it was just then that the Angel stirred. Sitting on his precarious bedstead he peered through the area railings.

They called the boy Angel because of the deformity of one shoulder blade. His legs were crooked too. They say his father had thrown him down the stairs. His face was twisted and wizened, but his eyes, - they were innocent as a baby's.

Those eyes now met a pair of heavy black boots, travelled up a rumpled trouser leg and soiled anorak, until they rested on Sam Huckett's face.

Angel did not notice the ugliness of its rage. He had recognised a friend. 'Sam!' he shouted.

Sam strode purposefully, if unsteadily on towards his victim, but the child was not to be ignored. With swift, spider like movement he hopped and crawled, up the steps and across the pavement, catching firmly hold of Sam's leg so that he could go no further.

'Me pipe, Sam! Yer got me pipe? Yer promised me, Sam - a little pipe like yourn.'

Sam looked bewildered. The meat cleaver fell to his side. Gradually recognition dawned. 'Why, if it ain't me little old Angel.'

'I bin waiting fer yer, Sam,' the child pleaded. 'Yer promised to make me a pipe like yourn.'

Taking the meat cleaver from his hand, Sidney had Sam gently by the arm. 'Come to the shop, Sam. You can use my tools. Here, Angel, nip down to the baker's and get some sticky buns. Rosie'll soon have the kettle on.'

Sam had a gift with wood craft, and it wasn't long before the piercing notes of a wooden whistle could be heard in Hackstead Street, interrupted by an occasional giggle or a deep guffaw. Back in the Old George Joe sadly cleared his debts and made off. After all, you can't have a fight when an angel comes along to tame your bull.

'Angel'

I was always haunted by the memory: all of Hoxton Street, silent, watching, waiting, as into view came this man, a meat clever upraised. I had walked on purposefully, pretending not to see or even to be there. But what should I have done? It was in writing a happy ending for this awful story that I was able to lay this nightmare to rest.

THE LIGHTED WINDOW

I was excited, and a little nervous, as I stood outside No. 31. At last I was going to meet my 'lady of the lighted window.' I had on my gabardine, instead of the old duffle coat I usually wore when I was working. I wanted to make a good impression.

The door opened. 'Mrs Conway, I'm Susan Hodgson, your home help,' I began.

'You don't look as if you're dressed for work,' she snapped. 'Anyway, it doesn't matter. No, don't bother to come in. I'm quite capable of looking after myself. Here is some shopping you can do, though. And I'll expect the receipts, - and the change.'

She kept me on the doorstep while she went for her purse, and now slammed the door in my face. I stood there, stunned, feeling as if it had actually hit me. Yes, it was my lady. I recognised her profile, and the soft white hair. The softness ended there. Her blue eyes had a steely glint, and her lips set in a thin line. The wrinkles on her forehead were concentrated into one deep furrow between her brows.

She lived in an upstairs flat in the street next to mine. When I took the children up to bed I would look across our garden and see her seated at a table. Was she playing Patience, I wondered? Sometimes she sat in a lower chair by the window. She was reading, I supposed. Probably, like us, she had not yet been invaded by television. She didn't bother to close the curtains. No one could see her, - only me.

'God bless her,' I would whisper. She seemed so lonely. I liked to imagine her life story, and how she had been left a lonely old lady. I always did have a vivid imagination. I pictured her as a laughing, fair haired child, brought up in the country, riding her pony and loved by all. I had wandered with her until her college days. Out of her many beaus she had chosen an architect – tall, dark and handsome, of course. She had two children – yes, that is the proper number to have – leaving them in an expensive school while she and her architect travelled the world. But tragedy struck. Her husband died of some rare tropical disease, and she was left a widow, struggling to bring up her children.

They were grown up long since, of course. Perhaps they had had an urge to travel too. I hadn't quite decided on that. And so she was left – a lonely, sweet old lady, living with her memories.

I had been delighted when I had received the phone call asking me to work there for an hour on Mondays. But oh, what a slap in the face I had had. It was the third Monday before I even got into her flat.

'You can clean through for me if you like,' she conceded, 'My legs are bad.'

It was arthritis, I supposed. It didn't stop her following me around and telling me how everything should be done, and carrying on about the lackadaisical attitude of the British workman, which, I gathered, was meant to include home helps.

In bed that night I poured out my complaints to my Reggie.

'I guess that is why they sent you, Susie. She needs a big dose of sweetening. Probably a few more before you have given up. There must be something lovable under that crusty old shell. Maybe she was a fair-haired, laughing child once. I wonder what happened. Something must have gone wrong.'

We lay in silence for a while, our imaginations wandering.
'Anyway, Sue, I know if anyone can help her, you can.'
'How's that?'
'You found something lovable in me, didn't you? Look what a big tough guy I was. I even sewed on my own buttons to prove I was independent, until you got in through my guard. .'
I snuggled into his arms and was soon fast asleep.

The next Monday I told him, 'Right, I'm going to see if I can get through her guard and begin to sweeten her up.' I cleaned through quickly and did her shopping. When my time was up I suggested, 'I've got a spare half-hour if you would like me to stay and have a cup of tea with you, Mrs Conway.' She had never offered me one.

'Are you short of tea in your house?' she snapped, and showed me to the stairs. I wasn't going to offer again, but a couple of weeks later she set out a tray. 'Have you time for a cuppa?' she asked...

Gradually I felt the ice was beginning to melt. Yes, it was Patience she played. I never admitted I had watched her. We talked about the books she read. She had the large print ones from the library. We discussed asking for a transfer to a downstairs flat as she was finding it difficult to manage the stairs. Never once did she mention her past life.

One day she pulled a book from the shelf to show me. A faded snapshot fell out. She grabbed it from me, but not before I had seen a glimpse of a fair-haired, laughing child, riding a pony.

'It's my daughter, Janet,' she said, grabbing it from me and placing back into hiding.

'She is lovely, and so like you. I'm sure you looked just like that when you were her age. You must tell me about her some time. I must go now.'

I didn't want to push her, or sound too eager.

Little by little, the story came out. Margaret Jameson as she was, had had a happy home life until her mother died. Her father, heart broken, left her in an orphanage. She never saw him again.

From the orphanage she was sent out into the world, totally unprepared. They helped her to settle into a job and a bed-sitter. They had done their duty. No wonder that when a dark-haired young man with smiling brown eyes came along and told her he loved her she agreed to live with him. Here was the love and security she had longed for.

They lived happily until Janet was born. Then, while she sat at home with the baby, he was out on the town. Night after night she would wait up, unable to rest. As soon as she heard the key in the lock she would creep into bed, pretending to be asleep.

'He was so rough and aggressive in the home – his guilty conscience I suppose,' said Margaret. 'Because of him, as soon as she was old enough, Janet got a job and left home.'

'Where is she now, Mrs Conway?' I ventured.

'I've no idea,' she snapped, and blew her nose hard. I slipped away quietly.

Later, I learned how she had told her daughter she didn't want to see her again. 'I suppose I was so upset about her going. And I've had to suppress my feelings for so long, that rather than cry, I shouted at her.

'Then, when Tom died, I moved here. I thought I'd make a fresh start. But I suppose when you are over 60 it is too late. This arthritis is crippling me. I can't get out, and as you know, I'm not much good at making friends.'

An idea was hatching in my mind. I talked it over with my husband. My impetuosity often lands me in trouble, and I rely on his wisdom. 'We could ask the Salvation Army to trace her daughter,' he suggested. 'But put out some feelers to Mrs Conway to prepare the ground.'

I did. Margaret had come to trust me. I often called in as a friend. Sometimes we would have a game of Scrabble. We talked about Janet, - how old she would be now. We remembered her birthday. One day she brought out a Mother's day car Janet had made for her in school. She had kept it all these years.

'I'd give anything to know how she was,' she admitted one day. That was enough for me. We set the wheels in motion. I was so impatient, but at last I had a phone call from the Salvation Army giving me Janet's address. I spent hours composing a letter. Reggie approved it, and it was on its way.

Every day I would rush to the letter box to see if the postman had brought her reply, but it was on a day when my mind was full of other things that it came. I had had a rare day out. It was late before I got in – and there was the letter!

'Reggie!' I shared, when he got in from work. 'She says she is so glad I wrote, and she is writing to her mother.'

The next morning I made time to pick a bunch of daffodils from our garden and ran them up to Mrs Conway. I gave her a big hug. She was crying for joy, for her Janet's letter had already arrived.

'Oh Susan,' she gasped, when she got her breath. 'Do you think you could spare an afternoon to take me to the shops? I must have some new clothes. My Janet is coming to see me. And Susan – I've got three grandchildren! In the holidays she'll bring them too.'

We bought new clothes and arranged for her to have her hair permed. Some pictures and ornaments that I had never seen began to brighten that austere flat, while Margaret herself began to look much younger. Even the arthritis seemed to be losing its grip. Somehow she was turning into my 'lady of the lighted window.'

'The Lighted Window'

This was the first story I ever had published. I had been so sad when I was told that the sweet old lady I liked to watch from my bedroom window was none other than our Janie's Gran, a truly aggressive old soul. I don't know if God ever sent anyone to unlock her hardened heart, but I so enjoyed writing this as a prayer for her, and others like her.

THE SPECIAL CLINIC

Amma blew on the charcoal fire; made sure the stew was bubbling, then, painfully dragging her crippled leg, began to sweep the courtyard. Everything must be ready when her mother returned from taking the other children to the clinic.

Amma hated the monthly clinic day, for she was always left at home. She understood that she could not walk the mile up to the lorry road, but at least with being the only one left in the village, for the men were working on the plantation and would not return until all the palm nuts were harvested, she could go into the bush to relieve herself with out being laughed at. How she wished she could use the latrines, but she could not balance on the boards that stretched over the great pit they had dug. If only she were normal like the other children.

'You weren't worth a goat,' her brother taunted her. A goat? Would her mother have paid a goat for her?

'Didn't you know? The priest used a goat to make a feast to pray to the obosom for you. When they couldn't pay for the goat he took Akusia. They should have let you die. I'm sure she would rather be dead than be the slave of that horrible old man.'

It was getting dark. Amma was afraid. Her brother's taunts rang in her ears. Surely it couldn't be true. She knew that sometimes her mother prepared a basket and went to see her sister, but she didn't know why she was living in this other village. Could it be Akusia was unhappy and it was her fault? Was it her fault that she was a cripple? Oh, if only her mother would come.

At last she heard voices. 'Amma! Amma!' her sister shrilled. 'The sister says' but Mother hushed her. 'I'm dying of hunger. No talking until we have eaten.'

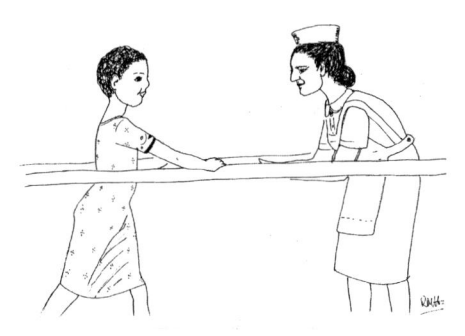

With deft hands she strained off the cassava and then whap, whap, whap, with their sticks pounding like piston rods, they mashed it up to make fufu. This alone could fill the void in their stomachs. At last, satisfied and sleepy, Amma dared to ask, 'What did Sister say?'

'Sister says she wants to see you at the clinic,' Afua chirped. 'That is right,' her mother affirmed as Amma looked at her, unbelieving.

The month passed. They made a little cart to push Amma along the forest track and then they all helped to heave her into the lorry. At last they reached the little market town where the lady from beyond the corn, with the white uniform and skin to match, came with her band of nurses and examined all the children. Amma's name was not in her book so she had to wait.

At last Sister called her. She looked at her eyes and teeth and tongue, and carefully felt her crippled leg.

'Amma, would you like to learn to walk, instead of having to crawl on the ground like this?' Amma's mouth fell open. She was too surprised to speak. Her mother's mouth was open too. 'Tell us how to find your village and I will send some strong young men to get her.'

'And so I felt that God was telling me that I must build a hospital and help children like you.'

Amma was surprised to find that there were other children like her, born well but then had this terrible sickness and after that crawled like lizards. Stomachs filled with nourishing stew, they sat enthralled as Sister taught them from the Bible. Now she is telling them how it was she started this special hospital.

'One day a doctor came here. By chance, he thought, but I know God sent him. He was very surprised when I told him I wanted to help you children. He knows a lot about polio, and said if I give you good food and teach you exercises, that you can come to his hospital and he will operate so you can walk again.'

'Please God, bless the good doctor.' They always prayed for Doctor Martin, and they prayed too for their own hospital to be built. They sent messages for all their fathers and brothers to come and help to dig the foundations. But – there was no cement. The cement came on a big ship, but it was still on the quayside when the rains came. Now there was a cement mountain on the quayside, but none for their hospital. 'Please, Lord, send us cement,' the children prayed.

Amma knew there was a God, somewhere far away, but did he care about little children being made better and about sending cement for their hospital?

She was so pleased to see her friends from the village. Everyone worked hard, and the children helped cook the food for them. They even fetched water by passing a bucket from one to another. But what was the use when there was no cement?

The village people worked for two days. The channels were dug, for the cement to be poured in, but they would not sit around and wait. There was work to do in their villages.

'Sister! Sister!' A boy ran up, a strange man following behind. Sister went to speak to him. Then she lifted her hands in the air and begins to dance about. 'Hallelujah! Cement! God has sent us the cement.'

After the work was finished the children heard the story. It seemed someone had 'greased the drivers palm', as they say, to bring cement to build his new house, but a land slide blocked his way. If the cement was not used straight away it would be wasted. 'Anybody want any cement?' he had cried, in despair really. He thought he had lost all his money, but this boy told him to bring it here. Truly God had answered their prayer.

Amma liked it at the hospital. The other girls were friendly. They had all been teased and rejected and now they all had similar disabilities, and were happy they were going to learn to walk and be like other people. She had a little bed to sleep on and good food to eat. There were toilets where no one could see or laugh at her, and there were bars she could hold onto and stand up straight instead of crawling. When sister had held out her arms to her she had even taken a few steps. But best of all she liked it when they had school. She could never go to school like the rest of the children in the village, but now she was learning to read.

'I am giving you each this special book. It tells you how Jesus, God's only Son, can be your friend.' The children were excited to have a book of their very own.

Amma treasured hers. She would wake early in the morning and read it. The fetish priest had told them God has many sons, and that the obosom that he prayed to was one of God's sons, but this book told her that Jesus was God's only Son, and that we must trust in him. Quietly, so no one would hear but God, she prayed the prayer written there.

Sister Meg told them, 'If you ask the lord Jesus, he will forgive you for all the bad things you have done. Then you will be happy.'

'Yes, God is good.' 'I have a friend, his name is Jesus.' The children sang and clapped their hands, and the nurses danced. When they were singing and praying Amma felt happy, but when she went to bed she still felt as if she had a stone in her heart. She thought about her sister, slave to the fetish priest. She had heard that soon that horrible old man was going to take her as one of his wives. If God could speak to Sister Meg, telling her to help them to learn to walk, couldn't he send someone to help her sister too?

God wants you to be happy, Sister told them. If something is making you sad, ask the Lord Jesus to help you.

Early, early the next morning, Amma crept outside with her little book. 'Lord Jesus, please will you help Akusia?' As she prayed she had a feeling inside her that she must give her precious book to her sister. But how? She did not know about sending things by post, and she had no money.

'Kofi, what are you doing here?' She had seen her brother prowling around before. If their mother had sent him he would not be skulking around like this. She knew that sometimes he liked to smoke. Surely he had not come to steal so that he could get money for his drugs? Amma tried not to think about that. No, it must be that God had sent him to help her.

'Kofi! Psst!' quietly she called to him and gave him the precious book. 'Will you take it to Akusia?'

'It will cost you.'

'You know I have no money.'

'I know that, stupid. Listen! I want you to do something for me. When the nurse goes and opens the office where they keep their supplies, you call her. Pretend you have fallen and hurt yourself, or something. That's all. If you'll do that I promise I'll take this to Akusia.'

Amma knew she should not do this. But she wanted him to take the book, and in any case, she was afraid of what her brother would do if she did not do what he asked. Sometimes he could be mean and vicious, not like her brother at all, but as if there was some evil power taking hold of him.

'Children, someone has been stealing the milk supplement sent us for the babies. If you see anyone prowling about, will you be sure to tell us?' Amma felt as if everyone was looking at her. Her face was burning. She felt ashamed, yet she did not dare to tell the sister.

'Amma, Doctor Martin is coming tomorrow to see if any of you are strong enough for the operation. You have been doing so well, and I know you are a brave girl. Would you like to go? Then you will be the first to walk, and the others will see you and work hard at their exercises.'

'Will it hurt, Sister?' Amma whispered.

'Yes, it will hurt for a little while, but afterwards you will be well and strong. You will be able to go back to your village and work on the farm and go to school like the other children.'

Amma liked it there at the clinic. They had good food and the nurses were all so kind, and best of all she loved the times when Sister taught them about Jesus and they sang their happy songs.

She lay on her bed and tossed and turned. She wanted to be able to walk properly, but if only she did not have this stone inside her, feeling so guilty that it was because of her that her sister was slave to the horrible old man, and knowing that it was her fault that the milk was stolen too.

'When are you having the opening for your new hospital?' the young doctor asked. He had funny white skin like Sister, and she noticed that he walked with a limp.

He was feeling the muscles in Amma's leg as Sister told him of all the answers to their prayers, how the bricks had been delivered, already paid for, and then a carpenter from one of the other missions lost his way and came there just when they needed all the interior fittings done and came back and worked until it was finished.

'Well, Amma?' he asked at last. 'Will you come to my hospital and let me help you to walk properly?'

Amma kept her head down. 'Do you know that at one time I was very ill? They said I would never walk again. Then a doctor came from a far away country. He believed Jesus could show him how to help me, and see; now I walk nearly as well as other people. That is why I have worked so hard to learn how to help you.'

At last Amma lifted her head and for a moment looked into a pair of grey eyes. 'I will come.'

Amma felt lost and lonely in the big city hospital. Many of the nurses spoke her language, but they didn't have time to stop and talk to her. After the operation she had to lie still.

The lady in the next bed was English, but when her husband came, he was an African like she was.

'Hey!' he said. 'You are both stuck in bed for a while. Why don't we turn one of the beds so that you can see each other?'

'Are you very sad?' asked Amma one day, after they had become friends, for Carry had such large sad eyes. 'Is it because you are afraid that you will be a cripple like me?'

'Oh no, it isn't that. You see, I had a little baby and he died. I thought it was my fault and I was so unhappy I tried to kill myself. I know now that even if I had done a bad thing, I was only making things worse. But your Sister Meg told me about Jesus, how he died for me, so I may be forgiven of all the wrong things I have done. She sent me this little book - see?' She held out the book. It was just like the one Amma had sent to her sister, Akusia, only she couldn't read the words. It was in English.

Amma pulled the sheet over her head and began to shake with sobs, but when a nurse ran over and threatened to move her to another bed she dried her tears. Then she saw that her friend had a pad and pencil and was busy sketching. 'What are you doing?' she asked. Carry smiled. 'If you promise to tell me why you were crying, I will show you.'

At last she handed Amma her pad. There was picture of a European lady and a little African girl dancing. 'That is you and me,' she said. 'I believe we are both going to get well and we will be so happy that we will dance. Now then - you must keep your promise.'

As soon as Amma tried to begin her story the tears seemed to well up, but she saw the fierce nurse looking her way and quickly blew her nose. She told Carry about her sister and the goat. She told her about the book and her brother stealing from the clinic. Somehow she felt better for having told someone but now she was amazed to see that the European lady was crying.

'Oh Amma,' she said, after she had given her nose a good blow. 'I can hardly believe this, but I am sure now that it was God who put us together in this hospital. You see, my husband is a lawyer, and he and some other people have been asking the government to make a law so that the fetish priests will not be allowed to have girls as slaves. I will ask him to see if he can help Akusia. But now, the first thing you must do is to tell the Lord Jesus about all these things you are sad about. Tell him you are sorry and ask him to forgive you. He will.'

Amma was soon ready to go back to their little hospital where Sister Meg could help her to exercise and learn to walk properly. She was so happy. She no longer had a lame leg to drag around, and since asking the Lord to forgive her, she had lost the stone she had felt in her heart. She helped care for the other children, and to keep the clinic in order too.

One day Sister Meg called Amma to come and sit beside her. 'Amma,' she said, 'I've just had a letter from a friend of yours. Do you remember Carry? She was in hospital with you.' Of course Amma remembered. 'She was telling me about some girls who were slaves to this old priest. It seems someone sent one of the girls a book, but she couldn't read. None of them could. So they asked a teacher to help them. Soon they were able to read a newspaper and heard that these lawyers were trying to help them. The judge said that it was because it came from the girls, that they were to be set free.'

'Would you like to meet your sister, Amma? She is coming here to help me in the clinic. She will be safe here, and she could train to be a nurse. And Amma, you will soon be able to go home to your village, but when you are old enough, what about you coming back to be a nurse too?'

It was a long time before Amma went to sleep that night. She had been so sad that her sister was a slave, because of her getting polio. Why had God let such a bad thing happen? But if she hadn't had polio she would never have met Sister Meg and come to her hospital. She would never have had the little book and come to know Jesus as her friend. And if she hadn't sent the book to her sister then she and other girls too would still be slaves. At least her brother had kept his promise and taken the book to Akusia, for all his bad ways. In a way he was a slave. Couldn't Jesus set him free too?

So many bad things, but good things happening, somehow because of them. She clutched her little book. Sister Meg had given her another one. It told how men had done very bad things to Jesus. But now, many wonderful good things were happening, all because of him.

'The Special Clinic'
This is the story, fictionalised of course, of Margaret Tucker and the wonderful work she did amongst the polio victims in Begoro, Ghana. I delighted in weaving in something of the story of Caroline, my neighbour in Oduom, and also of the eventual legislation bringing release to the young girls under the power of the fetish priests.

BEN'S BUNKER

Tom Griffiths knew he should have spoken against it, but he hadn't been prepared to risk losing his job. He'd worked hard enough to become the gaffer on the estate. Old Ben was harming no one, and in a strange way had become respected in the community, and besides, who else was likely to follow suit and build there among the sand dunes? But it was the Master's orders. The old hermit's home had to be demolished.

But now he finds his own son has befriended the old man. Would the family ever forgive him if they found out he had had anything to do with destroying Ben's home?

It was when he had seen Matthew's scrapbook that he realised someone must have shown him the secret places where the skylark nested and the fox had her lair, and the other things he had sketched so beautifully.

'I've told you not to go on the dunes on your own,' he roared, and then it came out that it was Ben who was his mentor. 'Matthew comes with me on a Saturday when I go out to the farm,' his wife intervened. 'Ben calls with fish and driftwood, and Mrs Jones sometimes gives him a meal. He took Matthew to see a plover with a broken wing, and when he realised how interested he was he showed him some of the other creatures he'd discovered.'

Jehovah Jireh

'Old Jones Jireh! She of all people shouldn't be giving charity.' They all called her that because of the text carved over the kitchen range, 'The Lord will provide.' Superstition, Tom said, but it seemed to have worked for her. Years before, when her husband had been killed with her boys still young he had urged her to sell up, but she had pointed to her text, and somehow the bills were always paid.

Well, whatever his family's involvement, the job had to be done. The tar had arrived. Ben's shelter, shored up with driftwood, was to be burned. Memories of long summer days when they had all camped on the dunes flooded back as he tramped over the sand to locate the bunker. He remembered their delight when as children they had tumbled out of bed and into the sea, returning to the aroma of bacon and eggs cooking on a drift wood fire. Of course there was the caravan park today, and even talk of holidays further afield, but he could not help but envy the old man who, having escaped from the dark dungeon of the mines had chosen to live out his retirement in the open air. A wisp of smoke revealed his retreat. Marking his route, Tom made his way home. Saturday! Ben would be up at the farm, so there would be no confrontation. Yes, he'd send the men then, while he would make sure that he himself was elsewhere.

Saturday came. The Welsh cawl had been left bubbling on the stove, and as soon as his wife was back from the farm she had lunch on the table. She was surprised to find her husband in communicative mood instead of hidden behind the paper as he usually was.

'Did you draw anything today, lad?' Reluctantly, his son brought out his precious scrap book, for his Dad had flung it on the floor last time he had seen it.

'What's this then? A bit of crazy paving?' He puzzled over the picture, until Matthew explained.

'It was a swallows' nest. I was so upset. It was all smashed to pieces. But Ben just laughed. He pointed up under the eaves. "No good crying over what's spoiled," he laughed. "It fell down so they just had to get on and build again. Eggs to be laid." Look, there's the new nest, Dad. And we heard the chicks chirping. They may be flying by next week.'

Tom Griffiths ate his cawl uneasily, then, instead of sleeping in the chair went out and began to dig up some waste ground that was always to be tackled 'next week.' Suddenly next week had arrived. He was conscious of a pall of black smoke away in the distance, but would Ben now be crawling back to the valleys, broken hearted, to live out his days in the workhouse? Maybe in some strange way the old man had been forewarned by the determination of the swallows and he too would just build again. Could it possibly be that there was something in this Jehovah Jireh business?

The next morning he sent his family to represent him in church while he went for a walk over the dunes. He had stayed away from the pub so did not know if the news was out yet. There was still smoke hanging in the air. He wouldn't go too near. Wandering near the shore, he saw him. Old Ben was far out on the rocks, fishing. Tom squatted down for a bit, watching him reel in his line. He was sure he could see a silver fish dancing on the end. Well, he certainly wasn't dying of a broken heart, and he would be having something for his dinner. *Had the old man in some way been forewarned and already dug himself out another shelter?*

Bethan was amazed to find her husband turning out some of his prized 'rubbish' from his shed. There was an old piece of carpet, some planks, and an old oil drum. 'You can get rid of these if you like.' He tried to sound nonchalant, but she knew well enough that it was an offering for Ben's new home further on in the dunes.

Next Sunday Tom Griffiths was all ready to accompany the family to church. He was going to be a better husband and father, yes, and gaffer too, from now on. Yes, yes, he might even think about reading the Bible. But somehow he didn't seem to have much of a welcome at church. The atmosphere was definitely icy, and it wasn't long after, in the market, that he heard someone pointing him out. 'That's the fellow! Yes, the one who had poor old Ben's bunker burned down.' He felt like Pontius Pilate.

So what had happened about all this Jehovah Jireh stuff? Could it be that there were conditions that needed to be met?

'Ben's Bunker'

This story is based on a real hermit who lived on the dunes around Kenfig. Since I couldn't find out much of the real story I enjoyed making up my own, and delighted to bring in the parable of the swallows, which happened in my kitchen porch in Ghana.

THE BLUEBELL

'They're on the run, I tell you,' Nell declared as they watched the Bluebell chug out of sight.

'Go on, Mother! You'll make a story out of anything,' Tom growled; unwilling to admit that he was curious too.

Nell had run to put on the kettle once the narrow boat had been sighted, for its owners were old friends, and would always come in for a cup of tea as soon as they were through the lock. But where were Ben and Annie, and who was this long haired, incompetent couple struggling to manoeuvre the craft?

'Ben was so upset about Annie having to go into hospital that he was glad to let the Bluebell go,' Nell volunteered over her knitting, as she sat beside her husband in the evening sunshine. Long since retired as official lock keeper, they had lived on in the cottage, and there was not a craft went through without his help. A month had passed, and Nell had had on her Sherlock Holmes cap.

'It seems he was tidying her up, and these youngsters up on the road watching. "Want to buy her?" he called out, all on the spur of the moment, and it was done.'

'But you don't have to make a mystery out of it,' Tom replied, after a puff at his pipe. 'Guess they just wanted to set up home, and this was a chance for them.'

'You mark my words, they're on the run.' Nell was adamant.

'They never go into the local shops,' she reported, a few days later. 'They'd rather walk a mile into the city than have people ask them questions.'

'Go on now, Mother,' Tom teased. 'They're only saving their pennies. Leave them alone.' But Nell couldn't or wouldn't. Then Mike, from the marina, called in.

'They've made themselves right handy around the place,' he told them. 'Self appointed protectors of our swans, and she makes real pretty pictures out of feathers and thistle down and the like. I said we would take orders, even offered them a job, but it seems I frightened them off. Next morning the Bluebell was gone.'

'Now then, Mother,' Tom cautioned, forestalling the inevitable "Told you so,' from Nell.

'Tom, I wish we could help them,' she confided, when Mike had gone. 'It's laughable really, if they are on the run, that they should come to the canals, for everyone knows everybody here. But all the same, it's sad. Running away never did any good. You have to face up to things in the end.'

'Tell them, then, not me,' growled her husband.

'I would if I got half a chance,' but Tom had escaped to his cabbage patch.

'I thought the Bluebell would have been through today,' he remarked, some weeks later. Winter was drawing on, and there were not many boats on the canal. 'I heard she was on her way.'

The curtains were drawn, and Tom in the bath when Nell heard the rattle of the lock gates. Surely no one would come through at night. As she ran out she heard a scream. A woman was struggling in the swirling waters of the lock, while her husband frantically sought to keep the boat from crushing her.

'Tom! Tom!' Nell screamed, rushing to their aid.

'I knew you were in trouble from the start,' the old woman confided as, dried, and her feet in a mustard bath, the lass was enjoying a mug of tea. Tom had been packed off to the Bluebell.

'I don't know what it is, but most troubles are not half as bad if you face them. You can't run for ever, you know. And you are going to need a home for your little one,' she added with a knowing glance.

'It was my fault.' It came tumbling out now, the sad story of how, discontented with their bed sit, Ellen had nagged Peter to get the deposit for a mortgage. He had a steady job, with the chance of promotion. It would all have come in time, but when there was this money just lying there, unaccounted for, it seemed as if it was the answer to all his worries.

'Instead, it was the beginning,' she sobbed. 'We didn't dare go to the estate agent, and we've been afraid to look over our shoulders in case a policeman was about to arrest us. Pete wanted to go back and own up, but I wouldn't let him. I couldn't bear to have him shut up in prison.'

'Oh, Tom! What have I done?' Nell groaned, as they sat waiting for some news. 'Oh, maybe I shouldn't have encouraged them to own up.'

Tom, as anxious as she was, couldn't offer any comfort.

At last there came the long awaited tap at the door. Ellen burst in, Pete not far behind, and threw her arms around Nell's neck.

'It's alright!' she bubbled. 'Everything is alright.'

Pete was the one who had to explain.

'My boss knew I had taken the money. He had felt so sure that I would come back that he had made it up out of his own pocket, so that nobody would know - and he's going to take me back; give me another chance. Oh, Nell! Tom! How glad we are that you persuaded us to go back and own up. We could have been on the run for the rest of our lives.'

'The Bluebell'

We had a wonderful, if strenuous holiday on the canals around Worcester. I was taken with the old man who sat outside his cottage and helped us through the lock, so had to write a story about them.

THE ISLAND

Flicking a wisp of hair from her eye, and blinking back the tears, Kate hitched her anorak closer to protect her from the teasing tormenting wind. At last she had captured the outline of the island onto her pad. Somehow the bleakness of the picture echoed the desolation of her own heart.

'Kate!' Andrew, her young cousin had been shouting to her, but now as he came close he forgot his message and peered over her shoulder.

'Hey! That's not bad. I like drawing and painting. There's an easel up in the attic, and a natty little case with paints and bottles and brushes in it. I wanted to use it, but Mum says I must wait until I'm older. But she might let you.'

'Did your Mum send you?' Kate asked, already folding up her stool.

'Oh, yes. Two car loads. She said would you come and help her to make some sandwiches.'

'Why, Kate! You're frozen. Warm your hands on this cup of tea. Here, I've put everything ready for you.' Aunt Mary continued to chat to her niece in between taking orders and setting the tables. Kate was used to the routine. She had accepted her aunt's invitation to come and stay, convalesce really, after her mother died, on the understanding that she was willing to help out in their little cafe.

'You could have sat by the window and done your sketching from there. No, don't tell me,' she laughed, as she bustled up to the urn, and then lowered her voice. 'You didn't want to be a captive audience.'

Kate gave a wry smile. It was true. She had never been a keen artist, but after a day of listening to her uncle droning on, putting the world to rights, she decided that she must have some excuse to get out of the house. She could hear him now, like some persistent bumble bee, talking to the visitors who had just driven up.

35

Well, perhaps they were interested in the Arab situation or the need of water conservation. She knew he had to stay near the car park in order to collect their money so she was safely out of reach on the headland.

'Mum, I was telling Kate about the artist's gear up in the attic.' Andrew came and dumped some crockery near the sink. It was Saturday and when visitors arrived it was all hands on deck.

'Why yes, you could use it and welcome. It was a distant aunt who came to stay. Someone had suggested it would be therapy for her to try painting, but she was really too poorly. She didn't even bother to take it when she went home. I've promised Andrew he could have it when he's older, but you could maybe give him a few tips.'

It was a fortnight later, and when Andrew saw Kate set out with her easel and case he was anxious to finish his chores and go and see how she was getting on.

'Hey! That's not bad. The lighthouse is good. You could have put a flag on the pole though. That would make it look more cheerful.'

'But there isn't a flag.'

'Well, Sir said we didn't just have to paint what we can see. We can paint what we would like to see. That's why painting is better than taking a photo.'

'Hum!' Kate dipped into a vermillion and soon a tattered flag was fluttering from the pole, demonstrating the skirmishing of the wind. 'Yes, I like that. Who is this Sir, anyway?'

'Why, he's a real artist. He has exhibitions and things. He's living near the bridge and he comes to our school and takes our art class. He's great. I'm going to be an artist too when I grow up.'

He must be great if he can fire a ten year old with enthusiasm, Kate thought. Then one of the visitors, noting her easel, asked, 'Are you studying with David Davies?'

Seeing Kate's surprise, she went on to explain. 'He has an exhibition in Jenkins, the furniture store in town. His pictures are so lovely we went in to enquire. It seems he lives locally, so we wondered if you were one of his pupils.

Kate explained that she too was a visitor, but when Aunt Mary's sister came in and also mentioned this David Davies she felt she wanted to know more. Her Mum, bless her heart, had realised how hard it had been for her to give up her teaching career to care for her, and she had so few opportunities now for building relationships, but she had believed that there was a Mr Right who would turn up for her daughter, somehow, somewhere. Kate, however, turning thirty, was aware that she had grown plain and uninteresting.

Now, don't go raising your hopes, she warned herself. You'll only be disappointed. Nobody's going to even look twice at you.'

She did go into town though, when her aunt offered her a lift, and together they went to see the exhibition. She stood there, enthralled. His paintings were somehow full of life, love and laughter. The children, playing in the foreground made you feel the tang of the salt air, the whipping of the wind, the grit of the sand between their toes. They were such happy pictures. 'Oh, I could love someone like that,' Kate thought to herself, and then she saw it. The little card with a telephone number, saying that he would welcome pupils.

Aunt Mary crossed the street from the supermarket and standing beside her, saw what she was reading.

'Why Kate! You must go! Let's give him a ring and see what he says.'

'But, I'm supposed to be helping you. And I wouldn't be good enough. And in any case, I've no transport.'

Mary steered her inside a cafe and ordered a pot of tea.

'Now, my dear. First of all, you came here primarily to get yourself well again. I had to manage before you came so, I'll miss you of course, but I could get by for one morning a week, even two. As for being good enough, if you were that good you wouldn't need a teacher.'

'Yes, but, how would I get in?' Kate tried to interrupt but her aunt was bulldozing all opposition.

'We could organise a lift for you with one of the tradesmen. We all help each other living out in the wilds as we do.'

Having squeezed second cups out of the pot she rose determinedly. 'Come on, m'dear. I've got some change. Let's phone now. I'll talk to him if you like.'

And so it was all arranged. A farmer who brought the eggs dropped Kate off outside a picturesque cottage. This was better than anything she had hoped for.

Of course she should have known that he was happily married. However had she allowed herself to indulge in fantasy? There were the children in his paintings. But this elderly, bearded man with black eyes twinkling at her from among the wrinkles had been so far from her expectation.

Oh, Kate! Kate! She chided herself. Just accept the fact that you are an old maid and get on with your life. But all the same, she had returned from her lesson with a spring in her step. David's wife had welcomed her into her farmhouse style kitchen and pulled a batch of scones from the oven at just the right time.

'Having students does David so much good,' she confided. 'We were delighted that you were able to come. He had a couple of others but they have branched out on their own. I suppose you will too eventually.'

Kate was amazed at how easy she found it to share her story and was quite relaxed when the artist joined them. He didn't bother about introductions. A mouthful of tea, a bite of scone, then wiping his hands he took her folder from her.

'The island! Of course, you're staying out there, aren't you? Oh, what a bleak outlook. Nobody would want to go there by looking at this.' He paused, finished his scone, his eyes searching Kate's face. 'Not too happy to be there, eh?'

'Now, now David.' Beth was anxious lest the girl were hurt. 'Kate's had a hard time. She came here to convalesce.'

'And we are going to help her aren't we?' A low laugh rumbled somewhere under his bushy beard. 'You see, we artists of all people are able to change our situation. We can dream dreams and then paint pictures of them. Dreams or prayers, call them what you like, but it's wonderful how situations can change if we want them to.'

He slipped into his studio to fetch a pad and began to sketch. Kate was intrigued when he showed her a girl, hair dragged back, sloppy jumper reaching over her crossed knees, as she clutched her mug. 'A little like you?' he asked. Amazed, Kate nodded. He continued to sketch, his wife clearing the table to make an excuse to look over his shoulder. She came and put her arm around the girl as he handed it to them. 'See any difference?' Kate was embarrassed yet delighted too.

It was the same girl. No doubt about it, but what a difference. Her hair was curling softly around her shoulders. She wore a dress, softly flowing to hide any gawkishness, and her lips parted in a smile as she gazed into the distance.

'You see what a difference we can make? And that's just with a pencil. I tell the children that there's magic in a paint brush. See things as you want them to be.

'Now let's look at your island.' They were in the studio now. 'Do you want to leave it as it is?'

'I've heard that monks used to live there,' Kate volunteered after a pause, 'and there were puffins. That must have been a picture worth painting.'

'Well, what about painting it as you would like it to be? Have you tried oils?'

He gave her a few tips on perspective and then left her while he continued with a landscape.

It was a good summer. The little cafe was humming with activity, for someone had seen one of Kate's sketches of the island and suggested that they put some in the local shops and hotels to advertise the place. The warm weather had tempted her into buying a pretty skirt and unconsciously she had taken David's suggestion of leaving her hair loose. Her aunt was delighted to see the change in the girl. Instead of resenting her uncle she had begun to tease him, affectionately dubbing him Uncle Bumble.

When a vacancy came up at her old school Kate felt that she was ready to take up her responsibilities again, but it was with regret that she said goodbye to the artist and his wife, and her family in the lighthouse cafe.

She freshened up her old home before term started and soon found that she had slipped back easily into the routine of teaching, and was getting involved again in the social activities of the village church. Somehow, since her return she felt a different person, enjoying her teaching, able to relate to people so much better. She had noted an advert in the local paper of an artist who welcomed pupils but she decided she had enough on her plate. The spare bedroom had become a dumping ground for her paintings. She was always intending to finish off the one of the island and hang it in her passage way, but somehow she wasn't satisfied with it as it was.

'Dream dreams,' David had said. Well, what is my dream?

It was in early Spring that she had the phone call. 'Kate, the most wonderful news.' She had to get her aunt to repeat it three times before she could take it in. 'So, if we can come up with some suitable plans, they will give us this grant?' All that money to be made available for their little outpost that seemed to be at the ends of the earth.

Kate went to borrow her neighbour's dog. He was a great companion on a tramp. Scrunching up through the beech woods she reached the seat overlooking the valley. Bruno sat panting beside her as she began to talk to herself.

'That's what we want, people to come and stay there to find healing and wholeness, to learn to dream dreams. But it's so cold there, and windy. However the monks survived I don't know.'

But Bruno, soon tired of sitting, was offering her a stick. She threw it a couple of times, then as she turned back into the woods she noticed the sun glinting on a conservatory built onto one of the houses across the valley. What a wonderful view they must have. Imagine breakfast with a panorama like this!

'That's it!' thought Kate. An extension onto the cottage, or maybe a separate building, with a few apartments where people could come and stay, and a sun lounge looking over towards the island. Why, it would be a tourist attraction in every weather - not just for Uncle Bumble to make money, but so that people would go away different, able to cope with life again.

The weather had risen to the occasion and Kate was able to wear her blue linen dress, her hair curling softly over her shoulders as she joined the crowds for this wonderful event. It had taken two years for her dream to come to reality. An architect friend of David's had drawn up plans that had been accepted by the council and a local builder had taken on the task.

The bishop himself had come to bless their venture, and David was there, autographing the prints they were selling of his painting of the island.

Kate was busy with her camera, trying to capture something of the scene, hoping that she might now complete her picture, when she was aware of someone standing at her elbow.

'You are Kate aren't you? David has been telling me about you. I'm looking for pupils and he thought you might be interested.'

It wasn't until long after that Kate realised how she had been charmed by the velvet brown of his voice, the ginger lights in his beard and his easy manner. Now she was just plain surprised.

'David? But he knows I'm just here for this weekend. I live in Surrey.'

'Yes, so do I.'

Most of the visitors had dispersed and there was hardly any tea left by the time they returned to the cafe.

'Well, Bryn, have you managed to persuade her to take up her brush again?' David asked, a twinkle in his eye. 'You know, I've a feeling she will not be your pupil for too long. This girl has got something.'

'David, why didn't you tell me that Bryn was one of your protégées?' It was a year since Kate had visited the lighthouse. This time she and Bryn had driven down together and David and Beth had invited them to the artist's cottage for tea.

'I was longing to,' Beth admitted, 'but David wouldn't let me.'

Seeing Kate's raised eyebrows the artist beckoned her to follow him into his studio. His wonderful impression of the island, with the monks rowing out past the lighthouse and the puffins gathered on the rocks had place of honour, but David picked up a pad and turned to where he had sketched Kate on her first visit.

'You seemed so sad and lonely then, and when you had gone I tried to picture you as I would have liked you to be. This is what came to me.'

'Oh David.' Kate found herself searching for her hanky as she gazed at the painting. There she was, just as she had been, hunched up with cold, trying to escape from the world as she sketched the lighthouse, but rounding the headland a figure was striding toward her.

'It's Bryn, isn't it? Oh, David, how did you know?'

'Oh, I didn't, my dear, I didn't. How could I? We didn't have any idea where you were living at that time, did we? Of course, once we knew, we did wonder whether something might work out but I wouldn't allow Beth to do any match making. You see, I dream dreams and paint pictures, but I believe in someone far greater who brings them to life.'

Bryn and Beth had joined them by now and David put his arms around the young couple. 'You go on painting pictures and you'll see, you'll bring sunshine into other lives.'

'The Island'

It was my sister in law who remarked that they could have made so much more of the place when we stopped at the little café in Anglesey. And I have never forgotten reading of the artist who painted prayers, so I delighted in weaving him into a story.

LOVE AND EAST-ENDERS

'Excuse me, but are you a lady or a girl?'

Helen was nonplussed by the child's question. She certainly felt immature. Nothing in her lectures, or in teaching practice, had prepared her for this onslaught of five-year-olds, some yelling for their mothers, others aggressive in their fear of this unknown institution, while yet others, like timid deer, shrank into themselves, too afraid to complain.

There was no doubt that Helen was a woman. Why else had she been so upset when she found out that Tony was courting? She had felt she must get right away from their close-built village, where she would be constantly reminded of her loss. What else but her womanhood could have driven her to apply for a teaching post in the East-end of London?

Not that there had been any understanding between Tony and herself. Tony was her brother's best friend, and had always been as one of the family. Tony had no idea how devastated Helen had been when he had turned up, at the end of his course at agricultural college, with a flashy sports car, and an equally flashy blond.

She had crept up into the attic with a broken heart. She could not think of a future without Tony. She had dreamed of teaching in the village school, until a family came along, of course; or at the farthest, travelling 20 miles to the nearest town, but always with Tony – her Tony.

About this time the students had to send in their teaching applications. Helen saw a letter pinned on the college notice board. An old student, now a headmistress, was writing, saying she was tired of teachers passing through. She wanted someone willing to stay a few years that would care for her needy children in London's East-End.

Deciding she needed to forget Tony and dedicate herself to her teaching, Helen applied. And here she was.

But it wasn't easy to care for these children. To start with, she could hardly understand them, though she did gather that the little Cypriot, who was offering fisticuffs to anyone who dared approach him, was not using the most tasteful of words.

A cheerful woman bounced in with a bunch of safety pins. 'Pin 'eir names on 'em, Luv.'

Grateful for the intrusion, Helen hastily cut up some card and soon they were all labelled. No one at college had given her a useful idea like that.

By the end of the second day she knew each child by name, and after a month she felt she had a class, instead of a mob of insecure individuals.

Helen quickly learned to use plastic pots instead of glass jars for the paints, how not to lose half her class in the toilets at the same time, and how to keep their Wellington boots from getting muddled.

She learned how to deal with biting, and bad language, and 'taking ways', though she could not guarantee her cures were permanent.

She stayed on for hours after school, trying to prepare thoroughly for each lesson. Then, surviving the chaos of the underground, she would make her weary way back to the flat she was sharing.

Often she longed for her mother's cheerful welcome, and delicious baking; the comfort of log fires and wide open spaces of the farm lands and the sweep of the distant hills.

It was nearly home time on a wet Friday afternoon but, with a rainy weekend ahead, Helen had nothing to look forward to. A group of parents were huddled inside the porch, waiting for their children. She bundled them into their coats and waved them off.

Returning to finish tidying up, she was conscious that someone was still waiting inside the door.

'Did you want someone? All the children have gone.'

'Aye, Miss, Ai've come for me little girl.' He laid on the familiar accent. The next moment she was in his arms.

'Tony,' she sobbed. She didn't know if she was laughing or crying.

'Father wanted some business done in town,' he explained, 'so I thought as how I'd meet you, and bring you home for the weekend. We're all kind of missing you.'

Strange, thought Helen. I've never known his Dad to have business in town before, but she didn't question it. She was so happy to be going home, and with Tony. No need to return to her flat to pack a bag. She had things at home.

But when they reached the station where Tony had left the car, she did ask questions.

'Tony, where is your MG? And what will Gloria think of you giving me a lift?'

Tony was sheepish. 'Well, 'tis like this. The car was expensive like, and so was the lassie. Seems like it was the car she was in love with. 'Twould be nice if someone would value me, not the car.' He gave her a wink.

Returning from her weekend with joy blossoming in her heart, Helen had so much more to give to her children. They began to feel more secure, and though, of course there were bad days when she felt she couldn't cope, she had such a sense of well being.

The head mistress was delighted. 'These children get so little love and care at home, bless their little hearts. They're like flowers in the sunshine with you, my dear. I hope you'll stay with us a good long time.'

'I'd like to,' Helen responded, sincerely, but her friendship with Tony was ripening, and they were beginning to talk about marriage. Tony was working on the farm with his father now, with the understanding that he would eventually take over.

'Why don't 'e apply to local council? Tha might even get village school. Old Annie won't go on for ever. Dad says he'll give us a plot. We can build our own cottage.'

Helen should have been thrilled. It was what she had always dreamed of. Why was she hesitating? It wasn't just out of loyalty to dear old Miss Armitage, though she knew how disappointed she would be if Helen only stayed her year, and it was bad for the children to have so many changes.

She wanted to have her own home and her own family. She wanted to marry Tony, but that wasn't all there was to life. She had to be herself, and here, among these little East-enders, Helen felt she had found herself.

'Tony, I'm sorry. I'm going back for another year anyway.'

He didn't understand. They passed the jewellers where they had planned to look at rings. There was a cloud between them.

When the new term started, it was Helen's father who drove her to the station. She was heart broken to leave Tony like this, but what a welcome she had from her children – no tears this year.

'Cor, Miss,' one mother confided, 'They've talked about yer all the holiday – their luvverly teacher. Play school all day long, they does.'

Six now, they were beginning to read and write. Helen didn't find them so exhausting, and had more energy to go out and about. She palled up with another teacher and they would go to the West End together. But still she grieved for Tony. He had been looking so pale and sad when she left – and hurt. It was she who was hurting him, and she loved him. What should she do?

It was the Friday before half term. Helen had planned to go home, but she was dreading it with this cloud between them. The children were gone and she was locking up the cupboards when a voice said, 'Be my little girl here?'

She started to say, 'All the children have gone,' when she realised it was the dear voice, the beloved reality of Tony, her Tony. But this time she stood nervous, questioning.

'Don't tell me you are up on business for your father again?' She had known it was a made up excuse before.

'No, for my father's son. Want to hear?' he held out his arms and gave her a hug. Helen began to sob.

'Oh Tony, I've been mean to you. I'm so sorry I've been hurting you, but please don't try to make me change my mind.' He silenced her with a kiss.

'Mean? Not my girl. I'm proud of you. Let's go and have a meal, for I've got something to tell you.'

At last she heard his story. He had applied for a job as a market gardener, in Essex. 'I wouldn't tell you until I knew I had the job. It's right near a station, so you can travel in by underground to school. Happen we can get a council house quite soon. Father has agreed to take on a manager for the farm, but if, by and by, we want to go back, the job's for me. Now, are you still determined not to marry me?'

After half term, the children gazed wonderingly at Helen's beautiful ring.

'Will you still be Miss Radcliffe?' they asked. A little boy held her hand confidently. 'I fought I was going to marry you when I growed up, he announced. 'But you'll still be my teacher, won't you.'

'Love and East Enders'

First published in Christian Herald, (this was their title – I can't remember what mine was) I have woven together my love of the little East Enders and that of my friend who so loved the Suffolk village where she had grown up. A bit of romantic nonsense perhaps, but I believe in happy endings.

46

THE PASSING PLACE

Cathryn breathed in the crisp air. 'And good morning to you,' she laughed towards the robin who was trilling from a thorn hedge, then paused to enjoy the lambs gambolling in the field beyond. Here was everything that a soul could desire to restore her life to tranquillity, and yet she had difficulty in fitting her key into the lock and as she slipped her car into gear she was conscious of the sweating of her palms, the too familiar tightening of her chest.

Why? There were no traffic jams here, with their inevitable pollution; no hassle to be faced at the office. She had left the high pressure of city life on her doctor's advice, coming to stay with her farmer brother and was happy in her work with an elderly solicitor in the town near by.

All your worries are behind you, Cathryn tried to tell herself, as she drove along the narrow lane. Another mile and she would be on the road. She glanced back anxiously at the gateway she had just passed. She could reverse into there if need be. She relaxed a little as she saw what might almost be described as a lay-by ahead. At least she knew she wouldn't meet the milk tanker. Yesterday she had been nearly frightened her out of her wits as she had rounded a bend to confront this monster. She could hardly have expected him to reverse, but fortunately had been able to squeeze herself onto the verge as he had lumbered past.

Cathryn breathed in deeply. At least now she was able to face up to the cause of her tension. Realising the problem was the first step to solving it. Wasn't that what her doctor had told her? Know your enemy? Something like that.

Well, she had been determined not to have to face Goliath again. Brian had assured her that the driver was regular in his timing, and all she needed to do was to leave a quarter of an hour earlier.

47

Breathe deeply! Relax! Cathryn opened her window to listen for the bird song, but instead she heard a gentle poop and the next minute she was head to head with a red van.

Bother! Brian hadn't thought about the postman. Or perhaps he had changed his route. Where could she pull in? Nervously she began to reverse. Where was the ditch? Oh dear, that was one thing about the city. You were seldom called on to reverse. It always had been her weak point.

Another toot, and she saw the van zipping back. As she passed him, waiting in a gateway many yards on, Cathryn caught a glimpse of a lean face beneath a mop of greying hair that broke into a sunshiny smile. 'Thanks,' she waved, embarrassed at being so inept. She was relieved to reach the road without further encounters.

'You are setting off more cheerfully these days,' her brother teased. Brian usually joined her for breakfast, having already finished the milking. 'Come to think of it, Alan seems to be full of the joys of spring too.'

'Alan? Who's Alan?' Cathryn asked, sharply.

'Why, our new Postie. I've never known him so regular in his timing, and he seems to be quite curious about you.'

'Now Brian. Enough of that nonsense. Surely you can pass folk on the road without someone imagining a romance. You had better work on your own love life. - Brian, I'm sorry.' She gave her brother a quick hug. Having recently lost, not only his wife through cancer, but the child they had so longed for, Cathryn knew that she should not tease him about such things, though she did long for his need to be met. But he should know that it was not kind to tease her either. She had been shattered when her wedding plans came to naught.

She had been quite choosy, but when she had met Robin on a rambling holiday she had been sure that he was Mr Right. She had been willing to wait for him while he finished his service abroad, confident in the assurance that they were both saving up and that there were wedding bells and a home at the end of it.

She had been shattered when eventually she realised that he had met someone else and was two-timing her. She was finished with men. Never again would she make herself so vulnerable. She had known that she couldn't stay with Brian permanently. He would build up a new life, and she must too, but meanwhile she had been so grateful that she had been able to leave her old associates with their pity and appreciated the quiet of life in the country, - apart from the trauma of passing traffic along the lane that is.

Alan. Is that his name? Who is he? She had heard enough of his voice to know that he was not local either. And Brian was right. She had lost her sense of apprehension and instead found that she was looking forward to seeing the little red van that was so skilled at reversing into a passing place. It was a month since their first meeting. One morning, instead of breathing a sigh of relief that she had reached the main road without meeting any oncoming traffic, she had felt dull disappointment, but then she had seen him coming up the hill. Their windows were down and a cheery exchange of waves had sent her happily on her way.

But was Brian right? Could he be interested in her? She found it hard to believe that, nearing thirty, and getting over a breakdown, that anyone would find her attractive, and especially under such circumstances. In any case, she was not available. She was determined not to allow herself to be so hurt again; and he wasn't young. He was sure to have a wife at home.

'I've left your breakfast in the oven. I have to go in early today,' she shouted to her brother the next morning. The Postie might be disappointed, but he would soon get over it. She was not going to get involved with anyone. Maybe it was time for her to think of returning to city life.

Her window was up, her radio on, so she had no warning of the approaching tanker. Her heart nearly jumped into her mouth as she rounded a bend to confront the monster. Where, oh where was the last passing place? In confusion, and yes, terror, she tried to manoeuvre back while the lorry revved up his engine and eased impatiently towards her. At last she reached a bank where she was able to pull in. She should have gone forward again so that she could have a better angle, but the tanker driver was pressurising her and so she edged in as best she could. With a grateful, or was it an angry toot, the driver squeezed past and lumbered on his way. Why, oh why hadn't she remembered that it always came at this time? How stupid could you get, she asked herself. She turned off her engine, tried to calm her breathing and wiped the sweat from her hands and brow before she continued her journey.

Switching on, she slipped into gear and made to drive forward but nothing happened except for the screeching of her back wheel and the mud that was being flung up against her recently washed car. It was no good! She was stuck! She didn't have a clue how to get out of this one. What should she do? Abandon the car and walk all the way back to the farm to get Brian to rescue her? By this time her chest was so tight that she doubted if she would manage it, and in any case he might have finished his breakfast and be far away over the fields.

'I'll do it my way' was being crooned over the radio. She snapped it off. Cathryn knew that she had been making a big mess of things, but was there a better way? She sat there, slumped in despair when there was a tap on the window. Of course it would be her Postie.

A cheerful grin. 'Looks like you need me.'

'Where - Where did you come from?' Cathryn, relieved, chokes up and searches for a hanky.

'Shove over!' A laughing Alan now; handing her his large and fairly clean one which she is glad to blow into – he slides into the driving seat while Cathryn climbs awkwardly across the gear stick. They sit there in silence until she recovers.

'Can't you find the key?' She tries to sound icy, but doesn't manage it and collapses into helpless giggles. 'Oh, I hate to admit it,' she gasps at length, 'but I am so relieved to see you. Well, where did you come from?'

Another tap on her window, sharper this time, and Cathryn awakes from her daydream to see, not her Postie, but a farmer from up the valley. He isn't best pleased.

'Better get out and let me get you out of this bog you've dug yourself into.'

It was this last indignity, and a phone call from a friend that made Cathryn decide to return to her life in the city. She didn't intend to waste her life living on day dreams.

It was spring time again. Cathryn had signed up for some evening classes and built up quite a round of activities that winter, but now as she came to visit her brother it was so good to breath in the sweet fresh air. Some practice at reversing with a driving instructor friend had made her less fearful of meeting oncoming traffic, and she was feeling more at ease about her brother too. With all the terrible pressures of farming and his personal tragedy, she had been quite concerned when she had left him on his own, but he had always assured her that he was fine, - when she could get him on the phone that is. If he wasn't out, his line was often engaged.

'Come on Brian, out with it,' Cathryn teased her brother, as they sat together over a cup of tea.

'I have you to thank for meeting Sally.' Her face was one big question mark. 'Yes, remember your Postie, Alan? He had come to stay with his sister, and taken this on as a temporary job. It seems he had had a skiing accident, and had to give up his job as sports instructor, and felt he had to get away for a while. Bit like you, eh? Well, soon after he heard that you had left, it seems he was offered a managerial position at the leisure centre where he had worked and decided to go back to his old circle.'

'But where does Sally come in?'
'Why, Sally is his sister. She had been widowed, about the same time as I lost my Jen. Alan was concerned to be leaving her alone and asked me if I might give her a ring now and again, or even look her up. She was brought up on a farm, and we had a few mutual friends. Once we met, that was it. We just clicked. As a matter of fact, I have booked us in for a meal at the Coach House. She has heard so much about you it is time we met.'

As Cathryn saw the couple, so animated and obviously in love, she mused about the strangeness of life. If she hadn't been so scared of passing places, and of getting involved in a relationship, then these two might still have been living with the pain of their yesterdays instead of building a new life. Surely it was something more than fate.

'By the way,' Sally interrupted her musings. 'Alan is coming tomorrow. We had thought of going to the horse trials. What about making a foursome?'

For a moment Cathryn felt her chest tighten, her palms sweating, but then she relaxed. Hadn't she learned to deal with passing places?

'Sounds good to me,' she responded.

'Passing Places'

It was over a mile from the main road to our beautiful Time Share cottage on a sheep farm in the heart of Wales. At first we watched anxiously for the passing places as we drove, but as the years passed we found we relaxed and trusted, and this made the setting for another 'happy ever after.'

FANTASTIC

'There's magic in these brushes.'

Gerald looked into the button eyes, just visible under his bushy eyebrows. The man's face was old and crinkly, reminding him of a lemon, ready to be squeezed, - though there was nothing sour about it.

'How can they be magic?' Gerry asked doubtfully. He was feeling so miserable that he wasn't at all sure that there was any magic left in the world. He hated the new neighbourhood where they had come to live since Dad had gone away; hated his school; his teacher who always seemed to try to make him look small, and the boys who took every opportunity to add to his humiliation.

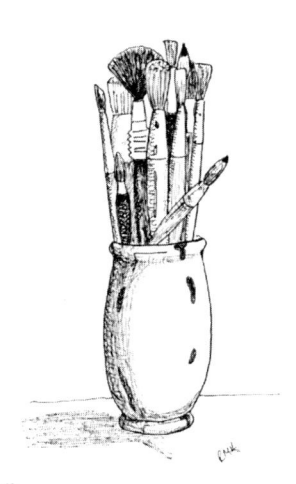

His Mum had come to visit a friend, and they had sent him upstairs to meet her father.

Gerald didn't need to be told that he was an artist. The large attic room was cluttered up with easels and tables filled with pots of paint. But now the old man pulled out an easel that seemed to be just the right size for a boy of eight. A low table was beside it, with all the paints that he might need, and he handed him a pot with a few brushes in it.

'There! See what you can do.' Mr Ford had turned away, humming to himself, busy with his own picture.

Gerald had always liked drawing. Perhaps that was why his mother had brought him to see the artist. He mixed up some paints. He loved the yellow, bright and shining. He would paint the sun coming up over the hill. He put some daffodils, peeping out from a hollow. There was a stream. The sun lit it up, all bright and gleaming. A silver streak turned out to be a fish leaping from the water. But then somehow big black thunder clouds came rolling in. He didn't know why he had taken up this large brush and begun to slosh it over his picture. Darker and darker it became until the paper was just one horrid soggy mess.

He threw the brush onto the floor, and put his head down. This was what always happened. Things would seem bright and shiny at first, and then everything would go wrong. Life was so black, so horrible. He wanted to get out of it, to run away, but where was there to run to? And of course, he couldn't leave his mum.

He raised his head, intending to tear off the paper, but as he did so he saw that among the thunder clouds there was a gleam of silver brightness. How had that happened? He thought it had all been spoiled. As he gazed, it seemed that somehow the clouds were rolling back so that the brightness made a pathway. Suddenly he realised that it wasn't on the paper. It was there, in front of him. Slowly at first, as if in a daze, he found himself walking along the path. Where was he going? What was he doing here?

As he wandered along he saw something glinting, gleaming. The sun was shining on a stream as it bubbled and splashed along, and yes, there were his daffodils. He crouched down to admire them, to see if there were enough for him to pick one for his mother without spoiling the clump when he felt something cold drop onto his nose.

'Oh no!' A big, black storm cloud was blotting out the sun. 'No! No! No!' Gerald was angry. Why did everything in his life always go wrong, always end up spoiled? It wasn't fair. He threw himself down, his coat pulled over his head while icy spears beat down on him.

'Get up, silly.' Someone was tugging at him, pulling him to his feet. 'What are you lying there for? If there's a storm you have to find shelter.' The girl was running now, and he found himself dragged along beside her, until they dropped breathless into a nest of dried leaves under a great oak.

Gerald looked at his rescuer now. She had little button eyes, but there was a shining in them, and her face was framed by tumbling hair that reminded him of sunbeams.

'But everything always goes wrong,' Gerald mumbled, as if by way of apology for his behaviour. He knew now that he had been stupid.

The girl took a mirror from her pocket. 'Look!' Gerry saw his sulky, sad face, all stained with earth and tears, while his black hair was sticking out in spikes as if he were some sort of hobgoblin.

'I couldn't leave you there. You were spoiling my picture. I like you in it, but we need to do something with you.' She offered Gerald a hanky and he began to scrub his dirty face, and then rummaged in his pocket for a comb.

The girl had left their shelter. 'Come on. That's better.' She took Gerald's hand and pulled him out into the sunshine. The only sign that there had been a storm was a rainbow framing the river.

Hand in hand they wandered along the path, through lush meadows and up into the hills where he had first seen the sun peeping. Somehow they seemed to be growing dark and forbidding, and then he heard it, - a muttering and sighing, and then mocking laughter. He pulled his hand from the girl's. 'I don't want to go any further.'

She turned and looked at him, her hands on her hips. He wasn't sure whether her little eyes were angry, or whether, somewhere, she was trying to keep back a gleam of amusement.

'Are you going to spoil my picture again?' she demanded.

'Me? It isn't me? There's someone, or something, - I don't know, that's spoiling it. I want to get out of here.' He turned and ran, and as he stumbled and tumbled down the path that had been so bright and sunny as they had climbed it, he heard the roll of thunder and felt once again the stinging of the rain. He pulled his coat over his head and ran, not knowing where, feeling only that he must escape from the darkness that was in the hills, the threat of the storm that was battering him.

A hand was gently ruffling Gerald's hair. 'Here, let's throw this one away. Haven't you found the magic of the brushes yet? Want to have another try?'

Just then Gerald heard his Mum calling. 'Time to go, love.' Excusing himself, he made to leave, but not before Mr Ford had called down the stairs, making her promise that she would bring her son again tomorrow.

The next day Gerald excused himself as soon as they came in the door and ran up the stairs to the attic. School hadn't been such an ordeal, for all day he had been thinking about the magic brushes, and the girl that he had met in his picture. Was it possible that he might find her again? But what about those hills that had proved so frightening? Did he want to go there again? But then she hadn't been frightened. Maybe he should have courage and face whatever it was.

Probably it was because he had not been looking miserable that the boys in his class had not bothered to bate him.

The old man was waiting. 'I hoped you would come,' he said. The easel was placed ready, but the boy looked at the brushes suspiciously. 'Are these the magic ones?' he asked.

'The magic ones?' he asked. He looked from the jar full of brushes to the boy.

'You gave me some magic ones,' Gerald told him. He was worried now. These weren't the same ones, he was sure. Oh, suppose he couldn't get back into his picture?

The old artist was laughing now. 'Oh, I remember, I told you there is magic in the brushes.'

'Isn't it true?' Gerald was on the defensive. He didn't like being laughed at. Was the old man deliberately deceiving him? Wouldn't he let him have them again?

The old man beckoned to Gerald to see what he himself had been painting. 'Of course it's true,' he told him. 'But the magic is not in any special brushes. The magic is in you. Want to see some of the magic that came from my brushes? Look!'

He pulled out an easel. When he saw the picture Gerald knew at once that it was supposed to be him. He saw a boy, buffeted by the wind and the rain, all hunched up, the picture of misery. Why would anyone want to paint anyone so miserable? He felt ashamed somehow. But the old man had another canvas in his hand.

'Now then. Ready for the magic?' The picture was on the easel now. Gerald gasped. Yes, it was the same boy. No doubt about it. But what a transformation.

He was a knight, in shining armour. His sword was held aloft, as if he had just conquered in battle; but he stood on a hill top..... Yes, it was the same hills that he had seen in his picture, the ones that had seemed so threatening. The stream was there, in the picture, and the daffodils, and in the distance, as if she were about to run into the picture to join him, was a girl with tumbling golden hair.

'You see, that is what you looked like to me when I first saw you,' the artist explained, 'but I didn't like the picture you made so I asked God to help me to paint a picture as he wanted you to be. That is a kind of magic, you know.'

Gerald was gazing, enchanted. He felt as if somehow he were there, inside the picture. He wasn't afraid anymore. Yes, there might be hard times, at school, and in his street, but somehow he knew he was a knight, and would fight and win.

'But, - the girl? She was in my picture...' She had been so real, and now, the old man had her on his canvas too. There must be some magic somewhere. Oh, if only he could get inside his picture again. He wouldn't let anything spoil it this time.

'Carol? But I thought....'
Just then there were steps on the stairs. 'Uncle Bill, I've brought you both a cup of tea.'
'Thanks, Carol, love. You know Gerry, don't you? Well, anyway, I think he knows you.'

'Fantastic'

I have always longed to be an artist, but I have to be content to paint pictures with words. I can't explain this story. You will agree that it is fantastic. Nevertheless, there is power in brushes, in words, in dreams and in prayers.

THE CHRISTMAS GIFT

'Oh, Geoff,' Lisa wept, 'I don't think I can face going to the Christmas service.' Christmas had always been such a special time for the Govens, since their Chris had arrived. Registered as Christopher, they called him Chris, their very special Christmas gift.

With Geoff from New Zealand and Lisa from Wales, theirs had been a fairy tale romance, meeting as they did in the highlands of New Guinea. They had begun their married life teaching in the mission school, with a view to returning to Geoff's work of Bible translation, but then, unexpected, a baby was on the way. Lisa booked to fly out to the government hospital to have him, but life was never predictable in the highlands. An earthquake and then a landslide, and the airstrip was out of action, the road impassable, and there were threatened complications in the birth.

It was panic or pray. Missionaries and nationals united in prayer, and God answered. From over the mountains, unscheduled and unannounced came a team engaged in a survey of leprosy, wonderfully, a gynaecologist among them. Their plans had been disrupted because of the earthquake and somehow they had been guided to this mission station. While the others managed to get home to their families, the doctor, an English girl, agreed to stay on until the baby was safely delivered - on Christmas Eve. The next morning Lisa lay beside an open window and joined in the anthems of praise which came from the church as they thanked God, not only for His Son, Jesus, but for another little child, Chris, another Christmas gift.

But now their only son was missing. Time had come when home schooling was no longer sufficient and Chris had been left with his grandparents to attend high school, and by now Geoff and Lisa should have been the happiest people on earth. For weeks there had been preparation for the celebration of his arrival for the Christmas holidays. They had been waiting to hear from the pilot before they rushed down to the airstrip when, instead of Bill's confident call there had been a strange voice telling them the plane was missing.

Everyone knew that flying in the territory was dangerous but the mission pilots were experienced in skill as well as faith, and had escaped from many a dangerous situation. All planes were called out in the search. It brought no comfort to be told that they had been flying over Kinabuli territory when they lost contact. If they had survived a crash there was little hope that they would escape these cannibalistic warriors.

Geoff had always planned to return to his work of Bible translation, but with Chris coming along, and a need in the mission school, the years had passed.

When they first heard news of these people, as yet untouched by the outside world, Lisa in particular, had felt that this was where they should be. But when a plane had flown in low, searching for a possible landing, these people had rushed out, shooting with their arrows. They had been glad to make a retreat, and the government had forbidden men to go in on foot until it was declared 'safe.' Only God could open the door for them.

At last there was some news. 'They have sighted some wreckage. It's on the top of a mountain. Yes, they are sending in skilled climbers to see what they can recover.'

'If they bring us his body, at least we will be able to lay him to rest,' Lisa wept. Geoff did not voice his fears that the cannibals might have got there first.

It seemed an eternity before they heard anything further but it did not bring them any peace. The bodies of the pilot and the couple accompanying Chris had been found dead in the mangled wreckage. Strangely there had been no sign of the boy.

'We must go to the Christmas service, love,' Geoff coaxed. 'The children have worked so hard, preparing.' He was going on to say, 'and what example would we be setting if we stayed away when we are in trouble?' but he glanced at Lisa's tear stained face and knew that he must not press her. 'It's OK honey. I'll go on your behalf.'

Lisa lay on her bed, exhausted by her grief, and once again listened to the toneless chanting of the hymns. She could visualise the children, unusually clothed in the Judean costumes that the missionaries brought out of their treasure chest each year, as once again they acted out the old old story of the first Christmas, and God's great gift.

The clear voice of the pastor carried up to where she lay.

'Let us come by faith to Bethlehem,' he called. 'Let us gaze on the child, and thank God for his great giving. He did not spare his Son, his only Son.'

For a moment she was carried back to the time she had lain there, her new born child in her arms. She remembered how in her heart she had given him back in thanksgiving to the Lord, who had given his own Son.

Geoff had been praying for Lisa throughout the service, so he should not have been surprised when she slipped in beside him. She did not hurry away when it was over, but stood outside the church as she had always done, receiving the embraces of the women and admiring their babies before they went their ways. 'Ann,' she called to a colleague, 'if it is not too late, we will accept your invitation for dinner.'

'Geoff,' she said, by way of explanation, 'It was while I was at home, listening to the service that I realised as never before what a wonderful thing God had done in letting his Son come to earth. And I knew that we have got to be willing to give our son, our gift, back to him. It has been wonderful to have him as long as we have.'

Together they knelt and thanked God for all the joy that Chris had brought to them, their own special Christmas gift. They still wept, but somehow the pain was eased.

It wasn't until New Year's Day that another message came through. 'We have been hearing reports of a white boy among the Kinabulis. We've got permission to go in. Does Geoff want to come?' Did he? But Lisa was more cautious.

'Oh Geoff,' she wept. 'What should I do if I were to lose you too? Of course you must go, but I am almost afraid to hope.'

Their guides had refused to accompany them once they reached the border of Kinabuli territory. It was an eerie feeling as the four men proceeded, calling out greetings as they went. They had been hacking their way through dense undergrowth for what seemed like hours, and had sat to rest and eat some of their iron rations when they were conscious that they were being watched.

'Hello! Hello!' they called, hoping that they sounded confident. A face appeared and was gone, then another, and another. They stood now to find themselves surrounded by fierce warriors, their spears held threateningly toward them. Geoff was conscious of the cracking of a twig, the rustle of a leaf, the faint chirp of bird, as the silence hung heavily around them. Had they ventured this far, only to be killed to satisfy these cannibals? Poor Lisa.

The silence was broken by a boy, about Chris's age, Geoff thought, who pushed his way through the circle of warriors. He was gabbling excitedly, one word oft repeated, - it sounded like 'tchi' and another word, 'kis'.

Geoff found himself being hurried along, the outstretched spears giving him no alternative, until they reached a clearing. Women and children were tumbling out of their little grass houses. They all seemed to have a grey tinge to their dark almost naked skins. There was gabbling and chattering as they circled the strange white men who had been brought to them. He searched them for any sign of a white boy, but before he realised who it was, someone was running toward him, leaping into his arms.

'Dad! Dad! I knew you would come. I knew.'

'Why, Chris?' Geoff asked when they had finished hugging and kissing and laughing and crying. They were seated now in one of the houses eating sweet potato that had been cooked in the ash. 'What happened to you? I don't know that I would have even recognised you. You are a real Kinabuli – an ugly one.'

'Why Dad, they all wanted my clothes. I couldn't keep them, and I tried to wash, but it was so cold that in the end I had to do what they do; rub myself with pig grease.'

'Oh - and of course this gray is the ash from sleeping near the fire.'

It was after Chris was safely home with his parents that they heard the rest of the story. He remembered they had been flying in dense cloud. They had all been praying, and then the pilot had said, 'Oh, blue sky. Here we go.' He must have thought it was sky, and instead it was the side of the mountain, was the only explanation. Chris hadn't remembered anything after that. The next thing he knew was lying on his back with brown faces gazing down at him and a great deal of chattering going on. There had been some vestiges of cargo, he remembered, still hanging in the trees, and these must have broken his fall.

'And then this boy, Bee, pushed his way through, telling them that I was 'tchi.' They all got excited then, and carried me back to one of their houses and gave me food and tried to look after me in their own way. I didn't feel afraid of them, although I wasn't pleased when they took my clothes.'

'But Chris,' Lisa asked, 'what does 'tchi' mean?'

'It means gift. They thought that I was a gift from the great spirit, because I had fallen out of the sky.'

'Oh Geoff, don't you see what this means?' Lisa asked later. 'I'm not saying that God wanted that plane to crash. I'm as sad as anyone else about the Baileys and the pilot being killed, but I believe that God sent his angels to carry our Chris so that he landed safely among the Kinabulis. He is a Christmas gift, not just for us, but for them too.

'That is what God did. He sent his Son, so that we may understand how great is his love for us, and he sent our Chris so that they know that he loves them too. Don't you see - we'll be able to go and live among them now, because of Chris.'

'Oh Lisa! Lisa!' Geoff didn't know if he was laughing or crying. 'I had been afraid to tell you. They would only let us bring Chris home on the condition that we came back. God so loved the Kinabulis that he sent his only Son, - and he has used our son, our Chris, as a gift to them too, so that they too will have everlasting life.'

'Christmas Gift'

When we were in Papua New Guinea we heard with great sadness of the loss of an MAF plane and the death of the pilot and of missionary families. That a child survived, cared for by these tribesmen who had previously met any attempt to contact them with aggression was a wonderful ending, and beginning of a story. My story is fiction, but based on these remarkable facts.

EAST, WEST, HOME'S BEST

'So, you're home again, Lassie.' The old fisherman puffed at his pipe as he leaned against the quay, his great coat pulled around him. He had expected the girl stepping off the ferry to be ready for a chat, but she strode on.

'I won't be staying,' she flung at him. 'As soon as Father is on his feet again, I'll be away.'

The wind was bitter and bullying. She pulled her scarf tighter as it tugged out a strand of her soft, sandy hair and slapped it across her face. Bowing her shoulders into its blast, she walked on.

Jeannie had left the island to go to college, and had never returned except for holidays. She had rebelled against the austerity of their life on the croft, and she wanted to be able to live her own life without being known everywhere as 'Tom and Betsy's lass.' And she certainly was not going to marry a crofter.

'If only I had married though, and had some commitments, I wouldn't have been expected to come now to look after Father. Even my job was not permanent, so I couldn't make that an excuse. I don't seem to have any roots.'

It wasn't that she hadn't had opportunities. A bonny lass, with a trim figure and a fresh complexion and she was full of fun.

'Maybe I have been too choosy. Here I am, nearer forty than thirty. They'll be calling me an old maid.'

Jeannie was fond of her old dad. Her mother had died some years ago and he had managed well on his own until he fell and broke his hip, never regaining his vigour.

She soon had the old homestead bright and cheery – a bed downstairs for the old man and everything planned for his convenience. They arranged for the stock to be sold and for someone to come in each day and see to the jobs around the place.

At last the bitter wind dropped and when Jeannie had finished her chores she called the dog and tramped over the hills and along the shore where she used to roam with her friends as a child. How beautiful the island was, in its own wild way. The fresh air brought a glow to her cheeks and a healthy appetite. Her father was soon enjoying meals such as her mother used to cook.

'I was chatting to the manager of the new hotel, Father. He would like me to go and help with the office work, part time. Do you think you could manage if I leave you some lunch?'

'O aye. I'll manage fine.' Tom was glad of anything that might encourage his daughter to stay.

It was a 'foreigner', as they called them, who was running the hotel. James Smith was a successful businessman, but his doctor had prescribed a quieter lifestyle, so he had taken over this venture. There were a few there from the mainland, and Jeannie enjoyed chatting with them about life down south.

One day Mr Smith had had a clash with old Petrina, who came in to clean. 'Oh, these Islanders,' he complained. 'They're all the same – as mean as old flint stones, and they stick together like a lot of limpets.'

Like a flash, Jeannie was on the defensive. 'You have to learn to be careful when you live on an island, and we need to help each other along.'

The manager's mouth dropped open. 'Why, Jeannie! I beg your pardon. I had no idea you were an Islander! You've lost your accent.'

'Aye, I've lived south for a good few years – and you can't talk dialect there. I'd almost forgotten I was an islander myself, but not quite, it seems.'

She had surprised herself at the way she had rushed to their defence. 'I guess I must have some roots still here.'

Father was improving in health. He was taking an interest in things around the house, but he was getting very demanding. Jeannie felt she was being taken for granted.

It was not one of her good days. She hadn't slept well and was cutting it fine for the bus. When Father complained about the way his egg was cooked, it was the last straw. 'I'm not your slave, you know,' she snapped, rushing out of the door.

She was still feeling sore by the time she finished work. 'Why should I hurry home? I'm entitled to some freedom.' She did some shopping, then called in on a friend for a cup of tea. It was a mild evening. She decided to walk home.

'Is it coming to the prayer meeting you are, Jeannie?' Robert, the young minister, caught up with her. He was on his way to the 'wee Kirk.'

'Well, I really should get back to Father, but I could come in for a little while.' This could be what I need, she thought.

Jeannie had been brought up in the Sunday School. She attended church once or twice when she first came home, but it was the old rebelliousness in her. Once she found father expected her to go, she wasn't going to be told what to do.

There was a homely atmosphere in the chapel. Each one gave a friendly nod to the girl sitting in the back. She was surprised to see their new neighbour, John Nisbet. He had come from one of the other islands, and taken over the croft adjoining theirs.

'I didn't know he was religious,' thought Jeannie. 'but maybe he didn't know I was either.'

Her thoughts wandered as they started to pray. She looked out of the window to the sheep, neatly sheared. Everyone knew whose they were. John was beginning to be known for his modern farming methods. What was it that had brought this young man to their island? He was thick set, strong as an ox they said, but softly spoken and pleasant looking. 'I wonder why he hasn't married?' thought Jeannie.

What was it had brought her back to the prayer meeting and a consciousness that she was in God's house? A young girl was on her feet. Her face was radiant. It was as if she were talking to the Lord face to face. Suddenly Jeannie understood. She was praying in dialect.

Perhaps the minister sensed that some did not approve. He was not an islander himself, but he spoke very simply of how our Lord, when he came to live on this earth, spoke the dialect of Galilee; and when he comes to us, he speaks our language.

Jeannie had much to think about as she hurried home to the old man. Her anger had all melted away.

He was standing anxiously by the window.

'I'll no be long the noo,' she called as she hurried to the kitchen.

Her father always talked dialect. How comforted he was to hear his lassie put away her foreign talk.

It was a good summer that year. They were busy in the hotel. Jeannie enjoyed her work. The peat had been cut and was lying on the hillside.

Then she came home one day to find her father lying on his bed.

'Why father, what is it? Shall I be calling the doctor?'

'Nae, nae, lassie. It's no the doctor I'm needing. You'd best be putting me in the home and you can away back south.'

Gradually she unravelled the story. 'Uncle Jem' the old neighbour, who came each day to see to the place, had said he could not carry on. Jeannie should have been delighted. The 'home' was not a bad place. A few of the old folk had settled happily up there. A visitor for one was a visitor for all. Wasn't this the escape she had been waiting for?

She knelt beside the old man and put her small hand over his old gnarled one. 'I'm no so sure I want to away,' she said. 'I'll speak to Robert. Maybe some of the church folk will give us a hand.'

They did give a hand. Jeannie often got home to find one of the neighbours had brought in a dish of broth and spent an hour with the old man. Young Sylvie, the one who had prayed in dialect, would put in a shovel as well as any, and took her turn, but her father noticed that it was always when Jeannie was home that their neighbour John Nisbet came to do his part, and Jeannie always managed to be there by his side.

'Father, would you not think it would be a fine thing if John were to buy our croft and farm the two together?' she asked one day.

The old man looked out on the windswept hills that he had known and loved since he was a child. He had been willing to leave the croft for the sake of his lassie, but now the glimmer of hope he had been hiding in his heart leapt into a flame.

'And would he be getting himself a housekeeper now?'

The flush on Jeannie's cheeks and the radiance in her eyes told him all he wanted to know.

'Aye,' he answered, 'It would. It would be a fine thing indeed.'

'East West, Home's Best'

This was also published in the Christian Herald. We had spent a wonderful fortnight in the Shetlands, and when a dear friend returned to her home there I wrote this story as a prayer picture for her.

LIFE IS FOR LIVING

Shiphrah's hands lay in her lap. Her long, strong fingers were twisted together in tension; those hands which were used to holding life in them. The woman was ill at ease, conscious of the drabness of her homespun garment against the bleached whiteness of the Egyptian women's clothes; of the plainness of her long black locks beside their perfumed coiffures.

The music of the harpist flowed on and on. Slaves waved palm fronds to stir the sultry air. Honey cakes were offered lavishly, while the sweet, persuasive, poisonous words of the vizier poured out, as his snake-like eyes held hers.

Ill at ease in the elegance of the palace, Shiphrah was only too aware that she was being conditioned – softened and worked over, as a potter kneads a lump of clay before throwing it onto the wheel.

'Think! Think what you can save them from. Better far to close their little eyes in sleep than that they should endure a living death.'

Think! How could she help but think. She was one of a suffering people, the proud Hebrews, whose men folk returned from the brickfields and labour camps, degraded, bruised and bleeding, to be tended by their sorrowing women. Her only son, her pride and joy, would limp home each night to fling himself hopelessly on his pallet and lie there until he must return the next morning to this hell.

What hope had she that she would ever hold her grandson on

67

her knees and know that their name would go down to posterity?

'Think!' he was saying, 'Remember!' He made sure she could not forget. What a shock it had been, their summons to the palace, she and Puah – the head midwives. Of course they could have walked there; but no. A chariot was sent for them. It wasn't by chance that they drove past the brickfields, and had seen the unspeakable horror – a young man being beaten to death. She knew it had been planned for their benefit.

'Oh God, where are you?' Shiphrah's heart was still crying with the awfulness of it. The harpist played on.

> 'How sweet to sleep within the mother's womb.
> Do not waken me to harsh reality.
> Close my eyes.
> Let me sleep on.'

'God!' her heart was crying. She believed in God. Since the time of Abraham her people had believed in God, a good God, a holy God, but – where was he? Oh, where was he?'

Could it be true that it was better for the newborn babies to sleep on? It was not the first time the midwife had faced this conflict. She remembered Mishcath, the baby whose face was so fearfully disfigured. It would have been so easy to let the sheet slip over him.

'Life is a gift. Always remember the precious gift you hold in your hands.' They were her grandmother's words. Their skill was passed from generation to generation.

Shiphrah did remember. Mishcath grew up. It was as though he had been given the gift of gladness to compensate for his deformity. How they all loved him.

Then there was Kachad. She had counted his little toes before she realised one arm was helpless. A proud Hebrew without a right arm? But surely he had a right to live. Perhaps he was thanking God today that he did not have to face the rigours of the brickfields – and how the women appreciated the strength of his one good arm as he helped them on their farms.

Then there was Marah, who had come to Shiprah secretly, pleading with her not to let her baby live, for her husband had died, and she was left with two unwanted boys already. But the older woman had kindled again the spark of courage in the heart of the girl, giving her strength not only to give birth, but to rear her children; and God had answered prayer and given her another husband.

'Life is a gift.'

They were before Pharaoh now – the two Hebrew midwives. They had known what he was going to say, even without the preparation of the vizier. Why else would he have sent for them?

'When you help the Hebrew women in childbirth, and observe them on the delivery stool, if it is a boy, kill him; but if it is a girl, let her live.'

He did not ask for a response. He had spoken. Who dared disobey?

Back home, Shiphrah prepared the evening meal. Fish again, always fish. Her legs felt weighted with lead and her heart was a stone in her breast.

An hour yet to sundown. Leaving the house, she skirted the village. She could not face the neighbours. She knew where she would find the old man. There he was, seated on a hillock, shaded by a tree looking toward the Promised Land. He lived on the promises of God; promises given to Abraham and Joseph. The weary Hebrews would often gather around him, while his words of life rekindled their faith.

Shiphrah sat at his feet. No need to tell him what had happened. There was little that was not shared in their close-knit community – their suffering drew them together. She sat quietly, unable to express her grief, reliving the horror of that death on the brickfield. Was life worth living? Should she save the babies to face this?

As if reading her thoughts, the old man spoke.

'He was there, you know.'

'Oh Father, if God was there, why did he not stop them? Why did he let Masah suffer like that?'

It was a long time before he spoke again.

'I cannot answer your 'whys' my daughter. Let it be enough to know that he was there. What they did to Masah they were doing to him. He was holding him, and taking the blows. Go in peace, my daughter, and know that he is with you too.'

Shiphrah did not go to the birthing stools for a few days. There were capable girls there that she and Puah had trained. She would be called if there were any complications. Even by not going she was disobeying the king, although passively, but at last she had to face the issue.

Natasha, Leah's daughter, was in labour. It was her first child. After hours of travail, at last the midwife held the little miracle of life in her hands. So puny and frail he was - a boy child. The mother had struggled to bring him forth. She would have to struggle again to rear him, and only to face the rigour of the life of an oppressed people.

Life, in her hands. So easily she could snuff it out. - Natasha, I'm sorry. He is stillborn. But he lived. Deftly she wiped out his little mouth, severed the umbilical cord, wrapped him in a cloth and put him in the arms of his mother.

69

They waited for the dreaded summons. It must come. They had defied the king.

Once again Shiphrah and Puah were in the palace. No chariot this time, - no special reception. The courtiers looked with wonder at these proud Hebrew women who had dared to withstand the king.

Shiphrah was afraid, yes, but she was prepared to die. She knew that the God who gave her strength when she was plucking new life from the womb, the God who had shared the agony of a young man out on the brickfields, would not forsake her. And she knew she would not die in vain, for she had a promise.

The old man had sent for Shiphrah.

'Because you have been faithful to him, God is going to bless you. Your daughter in law will bear a son and your family will continue through many generations.'

A promise! Her promise! What joy it gave her.

They are standing again before Pharaoh. What can they say? Their carefully prepared speeches have scattered like chaff.

'You have let the boys live. You have disobeyed me. Why?'

His voice is like thunder, full of threatening and impending judgement.

'Hebrew women are not like the Egyptian women; they are vigorous and give birth before the midwives arrive.' It was as if they had been given the words to say.

The storm has passed. He is conferring with his counsellors, already planning another dastardly plot to stamp out the Hebrews.

Shiphrah and Puah walk out of the palace – alive. They are alive. God has allowed them to live, and they must give the gift of life to others. To save life – this is their ministry.

'Life is for Living'

You will find the story of these wonderful women in the Bible. It was first published by 'Woman Alive,' when they were taking up the issue of abortion.

SHEPHERD LAD

Slamming the front door behind me, I made for my car, a scarf pulled over my head in protection from the keen mountain air. There was much to be said for the security of a nine to five job, but as I drove along the lane I lowered my window and gazed with longing across the rolling pasture, remembering my first sight of David, my shepherd lad, as I used to call him.

The wind had been ruffling his golden hair as it would a field of corn. The changing colour of the hills was in his eyes, and his smile. How can I describe it, except to say that it was like sunshine? No, he hadn't ridden up on a white charger. We had heard the unromantic pop-pop of a quad-bike as he approached, but now he had sat relaxed, astride his machine, chatting away as if he were a prince viewing his kingdom.

My parents had been abroad, and since taking a job in the county hospital I had been spending the occasional weekend with relatives. Returning from church with unexpected guests, after dinner Uncle Jack had taken us on a tour of the surrounding country side.

Heart of Wales they called it. I loved the wind swept hills and the sighting of a red kite lifting into the thermals.

'Oh Jack, be careful,' my aunt had warned as he had headed his Volvo up what appeared to be just a farm track.

'It's alright,' he had assured her. 'I met young Elton in the market, and he told me that it is one of the best views of the county up this hill, and that I was welcome.'

We had held our breath as the wheels spun in a muddy patch, then felt ourselves tipped back in our seats as it growled upwards, coming to rest at the brow of the hill. Windows were wound down. The air we breathed in Uncle Jack said came all the way from Cardigan Bay. The sound of an engine breaking the stillness would have jarred, had we not been filled with expectancy, and I for one was not disappointed.

Heart of Wales? Something had been happening to my heart. Crossed in love at the great age of fifteen, since then I had not had any lasting friendships, but here was someone of whom I wished to know more. I wanted to get out of the car, to shake my hair loose and say Hi, I'm Sonia; hop onto the back of his bike and let him drive me over the hills and far away, where I could hold his hand and look into those eyes, sometimes blue, sometimes grey. But I hadn't. With a cheery wave he had revved up his engine and off he went, not even knowing that I existed. Squashed into the back seat, he had probably not even seen me.

My aunt must have noticed how I would bring him into the conversation, this young farmer. She had made sure that I was there when she quizzed Uncle Jack about David. It seems that he had done a building job for old Mr Elton when David was just a little boy, and when they were admiring some horses in the market, he had made himself known.

Recently qualified, I had been enjoying my work as a physiotherapist, but now I had felt strangely dissatisfied and unsettled. Maybe I'd work out my notice and visit my parents as they had been suggesting, but when I had a phone call from my aunt, telling me about the quiz teams that would be competing in the village hall I forgot about Singapore. She didn't mention David, but there was something in her voice that made me feel sure that I should go.

David certainly noticed me that night. Somehow I was included in his team, and between us we made off with the cup. After that we didn't need a matchmaker. He couldn't spare daylight hours, but in the dark winter evenings we would meet up for a game of darts or snooker, and he promised me long walks over the hills once Summer came. You couldn't have said that we were courting, but we had a wonderful feeling of camaraderie and I was waking each morning with a sense of expectancy. Then, nothing. I didn't see or hear from David.

'I'm thinking of going to Singapore,' I told my aunt. She didn't need to be told that I had heart trouble. She must have had a chat with Uncle Jack, ever practical.

'You'll not be seeing David for a few weeks I guess,' he remarked casually. 'Lambing,' he continued, as if I had made the necessary response. 'They're at it night and day. Come May it should be all over and he'll have more time for friends.'

'By the way, have you ever seen lambing, Sonia?' he asked, later. 'We could take a run up to one of the farms if you would like.' He knew very well that I would like, but I wasn't sure that I wanted my aunt and uncle in tow. I set out in my mini.

There was no sign of David as I drove into the yard, but I could hear someone in the barn. I had met David's mother on the quiz night. A rosy, apple dumpling lady, now I saw her in a different light. In a waterproof and wellies, she knelt by one of the ewes until a wet little bundle of new life lay at her feet. 'There you are my beauty,' she purred to the mother, 'now you give her a good wash while I see to Emily here.' Standing up to uncrease her back she caught sight of me watching from the doorway of the barn.

'David's in bed, Sonia,' she called. 'He's been up all night, so I've taken over for a while. He must have some sleep. The farm is his now, but we always help out with the lambing. Here, come and see this little beauty.'

But I couldn't share her delight in this limp little lump of new life. I knew it would soon be gambolling in the fields, but this was as bad as the gory side of hospitals. I so admired doctors and nurses, but their profession was not for me, and neither was lambing.

We had sat together on the bales of straw while we drank a mug of tea and she told me something of the complexities of shepherding. I think she had thought that she was encouraging me to share David's life, for she had told me how he was always talking about me, but I came away weighed down with the dull pain of hopelessness. I knew that I could never ask David to leave his mountain kingdom, but neither could I turn shepherdess as his mother had done, making sure that he got his sleep while I turned midwife.

I was remembering how I had rung my parents that night, telling them that I was thinking of joining them, as I swung my car through the gate and moved up a gear, but all the same I kept the window open, listening, longing for that familiar pop-pop. Hearts are strange things, not easily healed.

I was remembering how my flight to Singapore was actually booked when I had had the longed for phone call. Some would say that fate had intervened, though I believe in a kinder Providence, and an aunt and uncle who were concerned for my well being.

A sleep deprived David had begging me to delay, to wait until he could take me on the promised walk over the hills, but I could not let my parents down and it was no good prolonging the agony. I could never be a farmer's wife.

Besides taking a temporary job I busied myself in the social life of the expatriates in Singapore. Mum and I had great shopping sprees, and they arranged all sorts of outings. The doctor blamed my poor health on the climate, and said that I should get back to Wales, and wonder of wonders, I had a letter saying that they had not found a suitable replacement and begging me to take my job back, and so here I was, back in the hospital, yes, with my predictable, nine to five job, and no messy lambing or mucking out. But my heart was still there, on the hills, with my shepherd lad.

At last I heard it, the familiar pop-pop. I glanced at my watch, then pulled into a passing place and waited. David came over the brow of a field, swung out through the gate and pulled up beside me. Our lips met in a lingering kiss before he spoke. 'I'm so glad I managed to convince you that you didn't have to turn shepherdess before you married a farmer. If nothing goes amiss I just might finish early tonight and we could go out for a meal.'

There was a joyous laugh in my heart as I drove on, remembering how I had thought Uncle Jack had been meeting me at the airport and then I had seen David waiting there. When I was in his arms we both knew that somehow, some way, everything was going to work out for us.

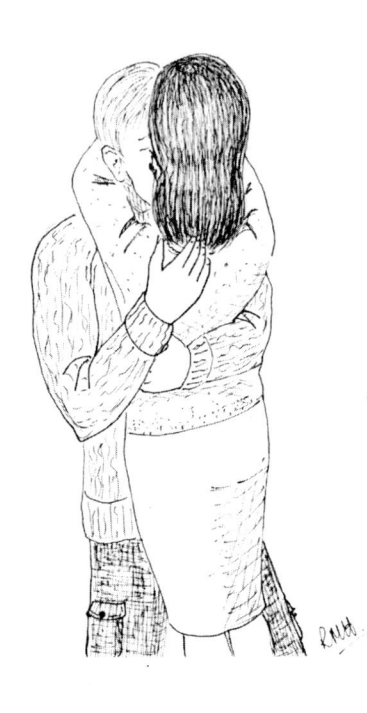

It seems that David's Mum had shared her concern for David with Aunt Jean when they met up one day, and between them they realised what the problem was. She had gone home to talk some sense into her boy, though he hadn't plucked up courage to make the phone call I had so longed for. Did Uncle Jack have to bully him into driving all that way to the airport? I'm not too sure, but I do know that we have had not regrets. Matchmakers they may have been, but surely in the hands of a kindly Providence.

I swung out of our lane onto the main road. Yes, I was driving on to my predictable employment, part of my heart still away over the hills with my shepherd lad.

'Shepherd Lad'

It was our dear friends at Llandrindod who had taken us for a drive up into these wonderful hills, when 'David' drove up beside us. With a sweet young nurse in the back seat with us, how could I help but write a romance?

SPRING OF JOY

'What is it, Tess?' Nell was busy putting in her border plants and did not want to be disturbed. Her collie would have been making much more noise if she had been feeling threatened, but she continued to whimper. Nell sighed as she struggled to her feet.

'Good morning. Can I help you?' The young man leaning against her low stone wall turned in surprise. He had been studying his map and had not noticed the elderly lady busy gardening.

'I seem to have lost my way. I was walking on the dunes. I thought there was a village nearby.'

'See the wicket gate?' Nell pulled out a rag from her apron pocket, wiping her hands before pointing. 'Turn right and you're nearly there.'

He heaved his rucksack onto his back, picked up the stick he must have cut from a hedge and thanking her, set off.

'If you're thirsty' she called after him, 'there's a spring in the dell over there. There's no water like it.'

Whatever made you say that, Nell scolded herself? You are just a silly romantic. But there was something about the young man. Perhaps it was his soft Scottish brogue. He was a long way from home as she had once felt herself to be.

She would have liked to have offered him a cup of tea, but she knew her niece would not have approved. She didn't like her living on alone in such an isolated spot. Yes, of course she must move, but oh dear. Nell sighed.

Her heart was following her hiker. There was something about his brown eyes, his tanned face and slightly receding hair line that had reminded her of her Tom.

Perhaps she should have warned him about the spring. But of course not. It was just their own fancy. She didn't want other people laughing at what had been so special to them.

In his thirties, her Tom had thought he was a confirmed bachelor. He had a picture of his prize cow where a girl friend might have been. He certainly hadn't been conscious that he was lonely, but his grandparents had cajoled him into drinking from the spring, and so he had drunk, yes, and wished, just to please them.

It was the very next week that he had met his Nell. She had been serving in the refreshment tent at the agricultural show. At the dawn of a May morning he had realised that there was a place in his heart that had been waiting for her to come and fill, while the Scottish lass who had given up her nursing career to move south to care for an elderly aunt suddenly felt that she was home.

Nell hadn't found the energy to return to her unfinished task. A mug of tea in her hand, she sat on the bench outside her cottage door, thinking of the happiness she had known with her Tom.

It had been an overplus to have the cottage with the meadow left to them and to be able to return to the source of their joy when at last Tom had sold the farm. But now he was gone, laid beside their little daughter and it wouldn't be long before she would join them.

Come on now Nell. You're not to think like that, she scolded herself. You've plenty of life left in you. Yes, but all the same, the cottage and the garden was too much for her now and her niece worried about her living in such an isolated spot. It wasn't fair to Emma.

Tess had brought her lead and was looking at her hopefully. Not that she ever needed to put it on her but she always carried it just in case. 'Come on then, girl. But mind you, no teasing the ponies.' Nell picked up a stout stick, put some sugar lumps in her pocket and set out with Tess leading the way.

Her collie wasn't so frisky these days. She wouldn't miss the meadow too much if Nell did move into the village. But where would the children graze their ponies? That was perhaps the strongest reason why she was not willing to sell. She knew that if she did, their meadow would soon be devoured by yet another housing estate. No longer was Nell able to thrill to the ecstasy of the larks but she knew that their nests were in the grass and she still had eyes to see the cowslips and violets that had disappeared from so many other places.

Tess had led her to the spring and having drunk from the trough that they had placed there for the horses, seemed to be looking at her expectantly.

'You want me to drink? Don't you think I'm too old for that sort of nonsense, old girl?' But she stooped, cupping her hands to drink from where the water gushed from the bank and felt a lifting of her spirits. She laughed as she looked in the direction of the gate. She hadn't told the young man that it had been their kissing gate.

Nell's step was lighter as she walked back home. Somehow she had a feeling that things were going to work out for her.

The warmth of the sun did wonders for Nell's poor old bones and she enjoyed keeping her house in order and even bought some paint to freshen up her kitchen, but after a long dry summer the winter winds began to blow and Emma was on to her again to think about moving.

'I don't want you to spend another winter here Auntie. I do wish you would move nearer to me. Mr Tiler says he has someone interested in buying the cottage. Won't you let me bring him out to have a chat with you?'

'It's really the meadow my client is interested in,' Geoff Tiler explained when at last Nell had agreed to see him. 'He wants to set up a business. He says the spring water is worth bottling.'

'Can you imagine!' Nell exploded to her niece later, 'Putting up some old factory in our meadow. And they would probably pull down the cottage to put up an office block.'

'But Auntie,' Emma sighed. She had so hoped that her aunt would have agreed to sell. 'You can't stay on here another winter.'

'I know, I know, but I'm not going to sell out to some city slicker who would destroy the beauty of our meadow just to make money.'

The leaves were falling from the oak and the winter winds howling around the cottage and Nell getting more and more depressed until at last she agreed to move into one of the sheltered flatlets. Emma had been helping her to clear out the accumulation of many a long year. She felt broken hearted as she prepared to break up her home. She knew that the land would have to be put up for sale, her beautiful antique furniture auctioned, but she could no longer have a say in it, for they needed the money.

'Come on Tess. Let's have a last goodbye to the meadow and the ponies. It's no good. We are too old and have got to go.'

The wind had dropped, the Autumn sun warm as she followed the dog, but as they neared the gate she could see a young couple, who obviously knew it was a kissing gate. She was teasing him, not letting him through without paying the price, just as she used to do with her Tom.

Nell would have walked away, unnoticed, almost jealous of their happiness, but Tess had other ideas. Forgetting her age, she scampered up to greet them as long lost friends.

'Tess! Tess! Bad dog! Come here at once,' Nell called, embarrassed, but they laughed at the dog's enthusiastic welcome and came to greet her owner.

'Why, I know you, don't I?' Nell asked, for she recognised her young hiker. 'It looks as though you drank from the spring then.'

Why ever did she say that? She hadn't told him about the legend.

'I certainly did,' Geoff responded. 'We'd love to tell you the story. May we walk you home?'

He waited until they were seated on her garden bench while he began, 'I drank from your spring, and the water was so good that I took it to the laboratory to have it tested, and that's where I met Helen.'

'And my Dad was into bottled water, and thought it was worth going into business.'

'And I went to a great deal of trouble to raise enough money to buy the meadow. We had heard that it might be for sale, but the owner wouldn't sell.'

'So what brought you back here this morning?' Nell asked. 'Did you think you might get her to change her mind?'

'She?' Geoff asked. 'It - it isn't your meadow is it? Oh no, we came just to have another drink, because we have so much to be thankful for and this is where it all began. You see, if it wasn't for the spring we might never have met.' Shyly, Helen held out her hand to show a cluster of diamonds.

'But you wouldn't really have wanted to spoil this lovely meadow to put up some old bottling factory would you?' Nell was beginning to have mixed feelings.

'Oh, it wouldn't have spoiled it. Look, I've got the plans here. You see, it wouldn't need a large shed, though of course we would have had to make a proper road through. But the ponies and everything could still graze here.'

'So what are you going to do now?'

'Why, Geoff already has a little house. We'll live there and just carry on with our present jobs, though I would have loved a cottage in the country,' Helen sighed.

'Something like this one?' Nell asked. 'Like to look round?'

Emma thought her aunt looked ten years younger when she came in response to her telephone call.

'You see, I'd wanted to keep the spring a secret, but now many people will be drinking from it. They may not know the secret, but who knows what wonderful things might happen for them too. If they're as happy as I am they'll be rich.'

'By the way, will you take me into town one day? I have to have a new outfit. Helen says I'll be guest of honour at their wedding.'

'Spring of Joy'

It was Joel, an incurable romantic, who told us the legend of the spring. He may have made it up, but I thought it made a good story. This was another prayer picture God answered.

78

THE VILLAGE HERMIT

'Whatever will happen to Thomas Thomas?' It was Martha Evans, 'the Shop' who asked the question, so you can be sure it was passed on around the village. It was little enough the old man bought at the store at the best of times, but she had hardly seen him lately – he would starve to death! And his little garden patch, that had been his pride and joy, had not been touched.

'He must be ill, Nurse Jones, Bach. Can't you do something for him?'

'I'm retired, you know,' she snapped, but in the end Dr Rees prevailed upon her to call. He knew that if anyone could talk the old man round, she could.

Thomas Thomas was not really an old man. He had had to take early retirement from the mines because of his health, and had withdrawn more and more into himself. 'The old miser,' they called him, or 'the Hermit,' and let him go his own way, not realising it was they who had driven him into his tower of loneliness.

Norah Jones was reluctant to intrude on his privacy, but she knew someone had to do something and, as usual, that somebody was her. She set her cap more firmly on her now grey curls, which framed a rosy, weather beaten face, took her courage in both hands, and set off.

The little stone cottage stood alone. How the villagers had chattered and gossiped when Thomas had sold his grandparents' house and moved into this derelict building.

'The old miser, hiding away his money. And for what?' they had said.

Norah propped her bicycle by the gate, calling out as she negotiated the garden path and pushed open the creaking door. The kitchen was bare; no sign of food about, and, as she thought, no more than a glimmer of fire in the grate.

The man she was looking for was sitting, wrapped around with blankets and reading a book that looked as battered and worn as he did.

A scholar he was. At school he had loved his books. He had been tall and slim then, with a mop of black hair and deep set brown eyes. Norah Jones was younger than he, and remembered how she had liked the quiet, studious youth.

But he had always shied away from her overtures of friendship and she had let him go his own way, as had everyone else in the village. And then, of course, her Idris had snapped her up.

'Why, Thomas, Bach,' she greeted him. 'It's a lovely day. You should be out in your garden.'

'Yes, yes, I know,' he apologised. 'It's my leg that is troubling me.'

'Agh! That old ulcer again! You should have gone to the doctor long since,' she scolded. She saw to his leg, promised to get the doctor to call, and coaxed him to eat a little. At last she came round to the point of her visit.

'You know, the doctor could arrange for you to go into the home, 'she offered tentatively. 'You'd get good meals prepared for you. No more housework, and you'd have plenty of company.'

'Company, Nurse?' He took off his spectacles and sat up. 'Company? No one has wanted my company all these years. They'll not be wanting *me* in the home.'

Norah cycled sadly home, thinking about the poor lonely bachelor who thought that nobody wanted him. And wasn't it true? Why, they only wanted him to go into the home now so that their consciences should not be disturbed.

He hadn't been wanted as a child. His grandparents had brought him up. Chapel people, they would do their duty, but it seemed they hadn't even bothered to choose a name for the little bundle of life their daughter had dumped upon them. So Thomas Thomas he was.

He knew he was an outcast. Even had the girls liked him - as Norah did – their parents would not have approved of their friendship with him. So Thomas had remained, lonely and apart; until Stephen came, that was.

Stephen too was an outcast. He was from India, not so dark in his colouring, but to the villagers he was coloured and apart. He had come to the university to study medicine, and he spent each holiday with the doctor in the village.

How Thomas looked forward to the holidays. He was 18 by then and already working in the mines, but in his time off they tramped the mountains together, or found a quiet nook and shared their books.

It was soon after Stephen had returned to India that the grandparents died, one soon after the other. Thomas sold the old family home and moved into this old stone cottage. 'Hope Cottage' it had been named. What a misnomer! And yet Thomas did not seem to be without hope.

He had always been faithful in attending chapel. There he was, Sunday after Sunday, until recently that was – not in the family pew, but right at the back where he need greet no one, and could slip quietly away before the minister could get to the door.

What was going to happen to Thomas Thomas? It would cause scandal in the village if someone should die of neglect on their own doorsteps.

Norah Jones had passed the word around, and Mrs Evans or Mair Davies would send a child along with a pie or a bowl of good Welsh soup. They didn't go themselves. They might see how much more was needed. Norah called in each week, although she was retired.

Then, one day, a dark skinned, refined gentleman drew up in his car at the village shop and enquired after a Mr Thomas Thomas. The villagers felt vaguely ashamed to direct him to Hope Cottage.

What curiosity was aroused! A few of them remembered the friendship with Stephen, so long ago. Could there be some connection?

A day or two later the young Indian gentleman returned. His wife was with him, dressed in a beautiful sari. Another time they came with their two children.

By now the neighbours were bursting with curiosity. They had managed to find out that the gentleman was a Dr Sanny, who had a medical practice in a nearby town. But what was the link with Thomas? Norah was sent, not unwillingly, to see what she could discover.

Thomas was out in the garden when she came. Together they went inside. The kettle was boiling on the hob. The little place had begun to look like a home. There was a cloth on the table and some flowers in a jar.

'Come then, Mr Thomas,' Norah coaxed, after they had been chatting for a while. 'Who are your visitors? I am dying to know.'

'You'll have to die then,' he teased, but he relented and diffidently related the story.

He told how, many years ago, the young Indian medical student had shared with Thomas his dream, not only to serve his people as a doctor, but to start literacy classes and teach the villagers the rudiments of hygiene. That was why, when his grandparents died, Thomas had sold the house and moved into a smaller place. He had wanted to share in Stephen's venture.

Week by week he had put aside most of his money and had sent it out to India. Some years later he received a letter telling of Stephen's death. He continued to send the money to his widow, so that she could educate her son.

'Why, Mr Thomas, bach,' Norah interrupted, 'We always wondered why you went into town so regularly. Walked too, to save the bus fare, didn't you now? But how does Dr Sanny come into your story?'

'Well, Dr Sanny was a friend of Stephen's family. When he came to U.K. they asked him, if ever he was able, to call and thank me. Then he got sent to Wales, and eventually settled in a practice in town, so he came.'

'He tells me that Benjamin, that's Stephen's son, is continuing the work his father started, so I am more than rewarded.'

You are being rewarded in other ways, thought the nurse, for she could see the old man was taking an interest in himself. But she couldn't help fearing what would happen should the Sannys move on and be unable to visit. Had he been lured out of his tower of isolation only to be left naked and defenceless?

Next time she went to call she could see Thomas sitting outside the cottage door. A girl of perhaps four years, and a boy a little older, black haired and bright-eyed, leant against him. He seemed to be telling them a story. A delicious aroma of Indian cooking wafted from the open door.

She went to pass on by but Thomas had seen her and beckoned to her.

'Come and meet my family,' he called.

'Your family?' she queried. Respectfully, she greeted each one.

'Mr Thomas is doing us a very great honour,' Dr Sanny explained. 'We have had to leave our children's grandparents in India. We all miss them very much. Perhaps that is why the children so enjoy visiting Mr Thomas.

'I cannot always take time to come here. Then the children trouble me too much. "When can we visit Mr Thomas?" So we are asking him to come and live with us and be a grandparent to our children.'

Norah called in at the shop as she cycled home. She couldn't resist starting the news rattling round the village, for she felt sure Thomas would agree to move in with the Sannys.

She called in to have a cup of tea with Mary Morgan. 'Just to think,' she mused. 'It took people from India to come and appreciate him. All we had seen was his crusty old shell, and inside he is full of sweetness. I'm glad he is getting some sweetness in return, after all these years.'

'Village Hermit'

James James was the hermit we knew, living all alone in his little wooden bungalow. I never learned his story, but I am sure that for him too, though maybe not in this life, there will be a great reward in heaven.

MAN'S BEST FRIEND

John didn't know about other dogs, but he never doubted that Cindy was his friend. Why, if it wasn't for Cindy they might never have escaped the meshes of the family.

With a bit of luck John might have Laura to himself on a Saturday evening. He could quite enjoy a concert, or even a lecture, if he had her beside him. There was always the reward of the walk home together. It got longer as the weeks went by.

Sunday was another story. Sunday was family day at Hazelwood Court. The Longtons were quite a tribe. John should have been forewarned; for he first met Laura at her sister June's wedding. There were endless aunts, cousins and in laws there, but John had only eyes for the soft-eyed maiden, her dark hair curling around her shoulders, floating in a vision of turquoise lace. John's aunt lived in the same town as the Longtons and, sensing a romance, regularly invited him for weekends.

For two years John had been coming, weekend after weekend, but still no sound of wedding bells. He would turn up at the family home on a Sunday morning, hoping to have Laura to himself, but he would be left in the lounge with the newspaper with nothing but tempting glimpses of the girl he loved. She would flit through, setting the table, arranging flowers and generally preparing for the clan.

Every now and again there was a perfumed breeze and she was there, kneeling beside him, soft arms around his waist, petalled cheek against his. 'I love you John,' she would whisper, but before he could respond she had tripped back to the kitchen and the heart of the family.

John would groan to himself, tormented by these tantalising morsels. 'If only you were mine…….really mine.'

At last the clan would be gathered around a groaning board. John sometimes wondered if Laura wanted him there just to even up the numbers, for she was the only one of the four sisters not married. Of course, there was little Matthew now, gurgling in his pram, but Lisa was doing her best to even things up.

John endured it, knowing that after the meal he could rely on Cindy to do her part. Cindy was a Sealyham, with cinnamon markings. She had been a birthday gift for Laura, soon before June's wedding. Her parents had feared she might be lonely with all her sisters gone. Not that they were far away, for Sunday dinner had become a religious observance with the Longtons, of far more importance than attendance at the parish church.

Coffee had been served. The ladies were chatting over the washing up, but Cindy was now demanding her walk. Laura knew that if she did not comply, her yapping would wake grandfather who by now was enjoying his nap.

John was ready to settle down. Nearing thirty, quiet and studious, he was tired of living in digs and of the long drive each weekend. He wanted his own home, and he wanted to share it with Laura.

It wasn't that they didn't talk about marriage. Laura had worn a ring long since. She was happy to discuss the service, bridesmaids, guests, but name the day she would not. She was confident that if she delayed long enough John would relent and move nearer. But John was thankful he could not get suitable work locally. He had a good job and was in line for a managerial position, and he needed to know that he came first in Laura's heart and life, not that he would be just a desirable extension to the family.

Laura had walked with her big, lovable John all through a bitter winter. The keen winds of March blew throughout April and then, early in May Spring burst upon them in breathtaking loveliness. The couple walk, their arms around each other's waists as they drink in the beauty all around them. Bluebells carpet the woodland and hawthorn adorns the hedges. It is when they reach their usual path through the meadow beside the river that John breaks into the beauty by bringing up the issue of the wedding. But worse, oh, much worse.

'Listen Laura,' he commands. 'I've got something to tell you.'

'What is it, John?' She slips away from him, startled by the aggression in his voice, but he catches hold of her hand.

'I love you, Laura. There is no one else in my life. You know that. I want you to marry me.' She snuggles up against him, coaxing.

'John, John. Of course I will marry you darling. I love you.'

This time it was he who drew away from her. 'I need a wife, Laura. I'm not prepared to go on waiting. We could have had a home and even a family by now, where I am. We'd still have been within reach of your family.

'Well – I've been offered promotion. The firm is opening a new factory and the manager's job is for me. I want you to come with me Laura.' He drew her close and kissed her passionately.

He hadn't chosen a very good place. Some girls passed by, giggling.

And Laura was not to be tempted into submission by kisses. She sensed what was coming, and Cindy now had left her search for rabbits and was getting restless.

'Where is it, John?'

'Shetlands.'

Laura is speechless, but not for long. 'That God-forsaken place,' she splutters. 'Why, you might as well ask me to go to the ends of the earth.'

'Some women have gone to the ends of the earth for the sake of the man they love.' He is gentle now, pleading. 'And remember, Laura, even the ends of the earth are not God-forsaken.'

'Give me time, John. I can't decide in a rush.'

'No, Laura. It is now or never. You've had two years to decide whether you love me or not. I would never have sought to go so far away – it is abroad really – but I'm glad that things have worked out as they have, for I'm not going to be kept on a string any longer.

'I love you, Laura. I want you to marry me, and I need to know that you love me more than you do your family.'

They had turned aside to a seat on the riverbank. Laura burst into tears, and clung to John, hoping to break him down this way, but he was adamant.

'There will be six months before I leave, Laura. Plenty of time to arrange the wedding, but if you aren't coming with me – well, it's goodbye now.'

All this time Cindy had been agitated. She would yap for attention, run off in hopeful search of a rat among the rushes, and return to bark more persistently, but she was forgotten. But when John and Laura stood up and started to walk in opposite directions, this was too much for the little dog. She was distraught and ran from one to the other, barking, whining, entangling herself in their feet, as if she were trying to weave a web to draw them back together.

Laura walked a step or two, choking back the sobs and scalding tears of anger and frustration, then turned to see if her John would run back to her, repentant and consoling. But all she saw were his slow but steady footsteps, though impeded by a small dog, going away, away.

Cindy was at her feet again, whining, pleading, as if to say, 'He's too strong for me. You stop him.'

Laura turned as the little dog ran off again, yelping piteously. John had turned too and Cindy stopped half way between them. She didn't know which one to go to and so she stayed there, crying, leaping as if in agony, as indeed she was.

An elderly couple pass Laura. Walking hand in hand, they are obviously very much in love. 'That's how we'll be when we are older,' thinks Laura, in spite of her conflict. They pause to gaze in wonder at the little animal.

'What's the matter with him?' the woman asks Laura.

'He's not willing for us to part.'

The couple laugh. 'I think you are meant to be together,' she calls back as they walk on.

'I think we are too.' Laura takes a step towards John and the next moment there is a flurry of two long legs and four little ones and the three of them are all tangled up together.

'To the ends of the earth, John,' Laura manages to murmur between a shower of kisses, and then,

'There is one condition.'

'What is that?'

'We must take Cindy.'

'Man's Best Friend'

Walking through this beautiful meadow, we stopped to watch this little dog, obviously in great distress, while the young couple attempted to go in opposite directions. Well, it does make a good story, doesn't it?

FIFTY YEARS ON

Jane notes the bemused smile on her husband's face, his head-set lying idle, even though the match is not over. 'Was that our Katie on the phone? What did she want?' 'An interview with her granddad if you please. Some school project, looking back to the beginning of this Millennium.'

Jane wipes her hands and sits beside him. 'There's lots we could tell her. What about the millennium bug? Remember Sophie stocking up on bottled water?'

Mark chuckles briefly. 'Yes, we teased her, but all the same you made sure that we had some iron rations, and filled the flasks on New Year's Eve.'

Jane laughs. 'And I thought you hadn't known. Now it comes out.' She tweaks his ear, then continues.

'All that doom and gloom about the computer bug, that all the computers would fail, and then it was the 'flu bug laid us low. Don't you remember? We missed out on Christmas that year. Why, what is it?' Jane is suddenly conscious that her husband is far away.

'Katie said they had to ask someone really old.'

'Well of course, when you're seven, everyone over twenty one seems old. Cheer up; we're only just out of our sixties.'

'Into our seventies, you mean. But it's true. You don't find many people reach their eighties these days. Where are all the old people's homes? It was the year 2,000 when they had discovered the secret of life and we were all going to live to be two hundred.'

Jane takes Mark's hand. 'We're still young at heart, aren't we?' He presses it to his lips. Their golden wedding had been a novelty to many, marriage an archaic custom left over from the last century, but it was their vows made before God that had held them through the time of Jane's breakdown. How thankful he was they had stuck together.

'Off!' Mark commands the all powerful television cum central computer. He might blank out the screen, but it is still monitoring their every move; for security, they are told.

They walk among their ecologically planned flower beds, part of this carefully arranged estate with its water recycling and solar heating systems. At last Mark is able to channel the turbulence of his thoughts.

'It's been so gradual we haven't realised what was happening, but it makes you wonder. All this fitness fanaticism. Has this increase of knowledge become a licence to bump off anyone who isn't a hundred percent? I know we still have our celebrity centenarians, but what of the others? And how many people have families these days? It seems a miracle that our Katie was born, after the pressure they put on Beth to abort the others.'

Jane leads him to a bench. 'Sit here and I'll bring out some tea.' So many changes, but they still can't do without their cuppa.

They would like to watch the sunset but the security blinds will soon roll into action. Every house is a fortress these days, for modern inventions cannot eliminate crime. Statistics show that it is escalating, and the gulf between rich and poor widening.

Jane sighs. 'It would have been nice to relax, wouldn't it? But we're booked in at the gym.'

After an exercise routine they are glad to rest. 'Oh Mark,' Jane whispers. 'It doesn't seem so long ago that we came here to have fun and work off our overflowing energy, but now we come because of doctor's orders. I guess we are historical characters.

'It's scary, isn't it? We didn't protest when they legalised voluntary euthanasia. It seemed a good thing, but you can't help wondering what pressure they're bringing and just how much of it is voluntary.'

Not expecting a reply, she continues, 'and all these 'child free' couples! They are so busy trying to produce the perfect society it's a wonder there are any of us left. But of course, that's no problem. Once they've found their ideal specimens they'll start cloning. It's bound to come even though we campaign against it.

'Oh Mark! I'm sorry. Whatever made me start talking like this? Of course - Katie. Us being history and all that.'

The following morning Mark lays an old shoe box in Jane's lap. 'Why!' she exclaims, 'The box we had when Tom was born. 1999. Of course, something to show our Katie, - the great interview. It's tomorrow isn't it? Oh look!' She holds up the silver crown millennium souvenir he had been given. 'We could show her this, and this one for the Queen Mother's hundredth birthday.'

88

'Katie won't believe that we had kings and queens. She thinks they're all the same as fairy tales,' Mark laughs.' What's this? Oh, Mark!' Jane unfolds the certificate they were given when Tom was dedicated and they had promised to bring him up as a Christian.

'Mark, what happened?' she whispers at last. 'We used to love to go to that church, and that was such a joyful service. We felt the Lord Jesus so near. How could we have forgotten?'

Settled in the garden, it is as if Mark is talking to himself. 'It's strange. It's only as you look back that things become plain. It must have been all this equal opportunities thing. We couldn't refuse to employ people because they weren't Christians, even in the church. Gradually we weren't sure who was and who wasn't, and...and - 'I see it clearly now,' he goes on. 'I must have known, deep down what I was doing, but I wouldn't admit it. I would never have got promotion while we were known as Christians, and there was the mortgage to pay and Tom's schooling. We didn't want him discriminated against, did we?'

He blows his nose hard, while Jane scrabbles for her hanky. Funny, with all this technology, they still need things like hankies. A buzzer sounds from his watch.

'Oh! Our game of squash. Better go, or they'll think that we're failing. Come on old girl.' Off again to the leisure centre. Armed guards are in evidence, even though it is daylight. Is it just for their protection, or is it to keep tabs on them too? Katie's message has unsettled them. They had entered the new millennium with such enthusiasm, a brave new world, but with all the progress of modern science they are beginning to feel that they have been trapped; like Katie's hamster, running in a treadmill. Since they have retired everything seems to be organised for them, holidays, social occasions and of course this intensive health programme. They have to prove their right to exist.

'Whom the Son sets free is free indeed.' The words distil into Mark's mind, and he speaks them out loud. They are walking quietly home, tired after their exertions.

'What are we going to tell our Katie? That we gave up our freedom, our faith, our Saviour, so that we might have the prosperity of this world?

'Prosperity, yes, for us, but the Third World countries are still ravaged by war and famine and disaster. And we have become prisoners of our prosperity.'

'Whom the Son sets free -' Jane repeats the words. 'Mark, it's not too late is it? Won't he help us?'

It is a sunny Saturday morning. Their grandson has breakfasted with them in the open air and left Katie with them.

89

She isn't as interested in the millennium coins as she is in the little gold bound testament, 'A Millennium Keepsake,' that had been among the treasures. 'You see, the year was so special because it was Jesus' birthday,' her Gran tells her.

'But why did you remember someone who lived so long ago? We don't remember Buddha's birthday, or Mohamed?' She is taught about the major religions at school.

'He isn't just someone who lived long ago,' Jane explains, drawing her near. 'You see, he had to die, for us, but he rose again, and he is alive today.' As she and Mark try to tell her the wonderful gospel story they feel their own hearts warmed; know that the Saviour is there with them, forgiving them, making them strong to live for him.

Katie hugs them tight. 'Oh Gramps, Gran, I want to be Jesus' friend too.'

'Mark, what have we done?' Jane asks after Katie's Dad has come for her. 'If she becomes a Christian she will have to suffer for it.'

'We used to sing about taking up our cross, but when it came to the crunch we failed.'

Jane squeezes Mark's hand. 'But it's not too late, and we must not deprive this next generation. Yes, they might live for two hundred years, but at the best it will be slavery. How much better to have a few short years, with Jesus as your friend, and - eternal life.'

'Fifty years on'
When a friend was asked to go and be interviewed concerning her memories of the war we were amused, but also challenged to think we are now part of history. But, stepping into a new millennium, to write about 'Fifty Years On,' was even more challenging.

I remembered how our niece had kept a shoe box of memories for her twins when they were born, and I hoped that our golden gospels, published as a millennial keepsake, might still be treasured in years ahead.

MOORLEYS Print & Publishing

We are growing publishers, adding several new titles to our list each year. We also undertake private publications and commissioned works.

Our range includes

Books of Verse
Devotional Poetry
Recitations for Children
Humorous Monologues

Drama
Bible Plays
Sketches
Christmas, Passiontide,
Easter and Harvest Plays
Demonstrations

Resource Books
Assembly Material
Easy Use Music Books for Piano and Keyboard
Children's Addresses
Prayers
Worship and Preaching
Books for Speakers

Activity Books
Quizzes
Puzzles

Church Stationery
Notice Books
Cradle Roll Certificates

Associated Lists and Imprints
Cliff College Publishing
Nimbus Press
MET (Headway)
Social Work Christian Fellowship

For up-to-date news, special offers and information on our full list of titles, please visit our website at **www.moorleys.co.uk**

Alternatively send a stamped addressed C5 envelope for our current catalogue, or consult your local Christian Bookshop, who will either stock or be able to obtain our titles.